Commander Rex and the Black Unicorn

Commander Rex and the Black Unicorn

Jesse Wilson

Copyright (C) 2018 Jesse Wilson
Layout design and Copyright (C) 2019 by Next Chapter
Published 2019 by Next Chapter
Cover art by CoverMint
Mass Market Paperback Edition
This book is a work of fiction. Names, characters, places, and incidents are the product of the author's imagination or are used fictitiously. Any resemblance to actual events, locales, or persons, living or dead, is purely coincidental.
All rights reserved. No part of this book may be reproduced or transmitted in any form or by any means, electronic or mechanical, including photocopying, recording, or by any information storage and retrieval system, without the author's permission.

Chapter 1

It is seven thirty-six in the morning. Rex, a man in his late thirties turned on his television and it was the same news story as it had been for weeks now. The trial of Pen Kenders droned on and on and there felt as if there was never going to be an end to it.

Rex didn't care if he opened the blade or not because he had real problems to deal with but still he couldn't believe what a mess it had made in Antacia all the same and now it was all these kingdom dwellers could talk about. "Do you think this kid did it?" Marion asked him as she walked out of the bathroom in a deep red robe. Rex took his gaze off the screen and to her with a smile.

"I don't know. It does seem kind of strange that thousands of generations of Blade Guardians happen, this nobody kid gets it and then the world comes to an end, or nearly, anyway," Rex replied to his wife with a shrug. "But it all turned out alright, the world is still spinning and everything is almost as it was before the disaster. It seems to me that everything turned out great," he finished and took his brown coffee cup out of the cupboard and set it on the counter.

"Well you were venturing in the Outside, hunting as usual, of course you didn't worry about it. The Northern Kingdom was a real mess for a while. We couldn't keep our eyes off the news," Marion replied to him and he got a cup for her too and poured them both a cup. "It was insane, we all thought the world really was going to end," she said shaking her head, still getting the chills.

Rex poured his coffee and turned around just in time to see Pen on the television, surrounded by media people and royal guards holding them back. He looked tired on the inside and out despite wearing a nice suit for court.

"Look at that kid, he's practically a noodle. No way he could pull one of the blades out, aren't they supposed to be locked anyway, ha, he didn't do it. He's just easy to blame. I'm really sure one of the knights did it, likely that crazy Giantess Knight, I mean her name is Miss Antigone. That's a ridiculous name," Rex said and got hit in the face with a wet rag and nearly spilled his still hot coffee.

"Did you forget that I am half Giant? You need to watch what you say, we're not crazy," she said and glared at him with her purple eyes that seemed to burn from the angle he was looking at her. Rex pulled the rag off and couldn't help but laugh just a little. "Okay, you're only just a little bit crazy," he said with a smile and she crossed her arms.

"I think everyone is a little bit crazy," she finally agreed with him and turned back to the television and couldn't watch it anymore, she turned the channel to one of her favorite cooking shows. "Ah look, Volente is on, she's making squid, I think It's squid," Marion said and crinkled her nose to this, she hated sea food and always wondered why she lived on the Borderlands of the Elroxian Kingdom. They loved sea food so much one would think that was all they ever ate.

"But she's pretty hot, I see why you like this show," Rex replied and sipped his coffee. "You are seriously pushing your luck, any more of that and I won't make your cream puffs the way you like them anymore," she replied and Rex's eyes widened. There was no way he was going to risk that.

"I understand, you win," he said raised his free hand in surrender. He knew better than to continue. She smiled with a nod. "I thought so," she replied and considered actually making some for breakfast in a little bit.

Rex looked out the window, the sun was just starting to come up over the horizon. The Western Kingdom was always the last to get the sun, but he didn't mind that at all, everywhere but the Morglands, where the sun never really got over the horizon and the unfortunate ones existed. His mind was wandering but his thought train was broken by the ringing of a phone somewhere in the distance, at least it sounded far away to him for a bit. Marion picked it up. The sound of the phone made him depressed, only one thing called this early in the day.

"Yeah, he's here hold on," Marion said and looked at him. "Hey, it's for you," she said and he looked over. She threw the phone to him and he caught it. "Thanks," he replied as he brought the thing to his head.

"Yo, what's up?" Rex said into the phone that looked more like a mini flat screen tv rather than an old-fashioned phone. He narrowed his eyes then "You're kidding me, are you sure?" he asked and waited with a quiet sigh to himself. "Alright, I'll be there as soon as I can," he said and Marion just sighed, she wished she could just break the phone into pieces and never get another one, these kinds of calls were always the same.

He clicked the phone off and set it on the marble counter.

"What is it?" she asked him and he took a much bigger sip of his cooling coffee. "Unicorn attack, small village thirty miles outside the wall," he said, never taking his eyes off the rising sun. "Oh gods, how many were lost?" she asked in a quieter tone.

"Everyone, not one living soul has been found yet I guess," Rex replied and knew that Unicorn attacks were becoming rarer in the modern age, at least until the Blade incident. There had been a spike in attacks in the following two months.

"I need to get out there as soon as I can," he said mostly to himself. "I know, just be careful," she said the obvious and he smiled. "If I was careful all the time I wouldn't get anything done but I hear you. I'll be back, chances are it will turn out to be a rogue razor horn or something like that. It'll be easy enough to deal with," he replied, pushed himself off the counter and walked back into the bedroom.

He quickly got dressed into his blue uniform, attached his golden unicorn hunter's badge on his chest. Took one look in the mirror to make sure everything was where it was supposed to be. He put his blaster belt on and tightened it.

"Okay, let's go to work," he said and walked out. Marion was waiting for him by the door. "You know the drill, if I don't make it back, will is in the safe, the combo is—" Marion cut him off with a kiss. "I know the drill, you get out of here and go make some four legged monster pay for this," she smiled and said to him. "You know I always do," he said and with a sigh he turned and walked out the front door.

The cool morning air shocked him awake and he walked to his car. He opened the door and got in, started it up. Some morning news radio started to come through his speakers.

"Hello good people, this is Bob coming at you live from radio land. Today the trial of the century continues. Pen Kenders is accused of opening the Mimic Blade causing the disaster of the Northern Kingdom as you know, what do you think? Call us right now and you can have your opinions live on the air," the DJ said and Rex winced, he was over this stuff and turned off the radio. That and he was never a big fan of Bob. He rolled the window down and drove off.

Marion was waving at him as he left, but he didn't see her as he turned the corner.

Chapter 2

The western kingdom was a wet, drippy kingdom and it rained the night before. Rex splashed through a puddle on the road as the natural mist in the air condensed on his windshield was wiped away by the wipers, he couldn't wait to get reassigned somewhere else. This place was made for Elxroxians, not humans or anything else, he thought to himself as he splashed through another puddle and felt his car slide on the road a little. He was just thankful it never froze over.

Rex drove down the water-logged road and looked to his left. There in the mist there was Brule castle, his destination. Rex made the rest of his quiet journey trying to put together a theory on why a whole village was attacked and wiped out. None of it made any sense, unicorns were dangerous but a whole town wiped out was extremely rare.

He rolled up to the gate and came to a stop.

An Elroxian stood there in her uniform in the guard booth her black eyes widened when he rolled the window down. "Rex, don't take this personal but every time you show up it's bad news," she said to him and he sighed. "I'm afraid that it's going to be one of those days," he replied as he said this he grabbed her Aquarian Star crest hanging around her neck absentmindedly. Understanding the tone well she decided not to press the issue. Her green, scaly hand moved to the button and opened the gate.

"Good luck," she said to him and Rex just smiled weakly as he drove through to the castle.

Rex got out of his car and a valet immediately came and he was given the keys. "Take good care of her, please," he said to the valet. "You got it, sir, as always," he replied to him as he got in the car and drove away. Rex moved his way into the side door where a woman was waiting for him.

"Alright, what is really going on here? Unicorns don't wipe out whole towns. They pick off one or two people at a time," Rex knew his enemy's habits and this didn't make any sense. "True, but we have a live drone feed from the scene, there aren't any bodies and the walls are scorched. The only evidence that people were there at all is their shadows burned into walls," she said to him and Rex was confused. "A Pyrehorn in the rainy season and under the sea, what sense does that make?" he asked himself.

"Yeah you're guess was as good as ours but that is exactly what it looks like," she said as they walked down the hall towards a door with two Elroxian guards posted outside, they opened the doors to a command center with people at computers and filled with people talking on their phones, to one another and people looking through old books for information.

"Controlled chaos, is there something you're not telling me?" Rex asked as he looked around the command center, surprised that no one even noticed he came in. "When the water is scorched, the black horn rises," she said and Rex heard these words before, a long time ago but threw it off as nonsense. "A ten-thousand-year-old prophecy, you can't be serious," Rex replied.

"Well if a Pyrehorn attacked an underwater village and killed everyone, what would you call it?" she asked him and with that the golden phone in the middle of the room began to ring, a high pitched ring that brought the room to silence as they heard it. It was the King's Phone.

"It's for you," she said and Rex just looked at her. "Yeah Bonnie, I got it, thanks," Rex replied, walked to the phone and answered it. "Hello," he said into the phone. "Understood, I'll be up at once," he said and hung it up. "The King summons me, does anyone have an Aquarian Star I can borrow?" he asked and Bonnie pulled one out of her pocket, tossed it to him. He caught it.

"Borok," he said and a chain appeared around it, he put it around his neck. "Thanks," he said and walked into the elevator connecting the two rooms. "Good luck," Bonnie replied as the center resumed its activity.

The trip to the inner chamber from the command center was very short. The elevator ride wasn't the problem, the stopping on the other hand was. The ride came to a stop and water began seep inside the thing. Rex hated this part, as a human he wasn't meant to breathe underwater but the crest of the star helped him with that. Soon the whole elevator was filled with ice cold water, the first breath was always the hardest one to take. His lungs burned but instead of resisting he forced himself to keep breathing. It always got easier.

The doors opened and he walked out into the crystal clear water filled chamber. A magical enchantment kept him from floating all over the place as he walked forward. The king was waiting for him. Not sitting in the Coral throne but standing in front of it. "Ah, mister Rex, it's always good to see you," Lexam said to him in a deep voice and continued. "I hope all is well?" the King asked and Rex smiled. "Yes, everything is great," he replied but he wanted to get down to business.

"What does all of this have to do with you? I can handle an insane Pyrohorn," Rex replied and the King flashed his black eyes at him and it sent a small shiver down Rex's spine. The Elroxian King could be intimidating with his thick green skin and imposing, tall stature. Rex was tall but the Elroxian King was taller than any human, just then Rex realized that this figure could have him killed for talking to him like this and didn't know where his mind was at for a second. The King's expression softened and he began to answer.

"I don't doubt your skills or your ability to handle this in the least. However, there is something that you should know," Lexam said to him and walked to the Coral Throne. "My father ruled the best he could, but the prophecy always ate at him. He was always afraid of what was out there sleeping in the deep black oceans where only the most foolish of our race attempt to go," Lexam said and picked up an ancient, scaly book that was sitting on the left arm of the throne.

"This book is thousands of years old. Every king donates their largest chest scale on their death to add another page to it. I'll do it and hopefully the tradition will continue long after I am gone, there are secrets in here but only one that concerns you," Lexam said and opened the book to a page near the beginning. "When the water is scorched, the black horn rises from the depths of the sea and all living things will be obliterated," Lexam said the only line that was dedicated to the page.

"I knew I heard those words before but, black horn, that doesn't make any sense. I've seen every Unicorn from every kingdom and area on this whole world. There aren't any pure black ones. I've done this job for ten years and trained in it for five before that, this is a myth," Rex replied, he was one hundred percent sure this was a story made up by some crazy King ages ago to mess with every proceeding ruler's head, nothing more.

"Myth or not I need you to investigate this. Pyre horns never attack in the rain, and underwater? Every school kid knows this. But this one did and I need you to tell me why. If this is real, everything we know is at risk. I don't want to be the King that goes down in history as the one who lets the Western Kingdom and world go to ruin," Lexam said to him and despite his imposing stature, Rex felt genuine terror coming from him.

"Don't worry. We'll look into this mess. I haven't met a unicorn yet I couldn't banish," Rex said with a smile, confident that this unicorn story was nothing more than an effect of the blades being unleashed and things were just out of balance is all. "You have all the resources of the Kingdom at your disposal, all you need do is ask," Lexam said to him and Rex smiled. "I'll need my ship, if this is as big of a problem as you say we're going to need the whole crew," Rex replied, but he didn't want to get greedy here. It could have been some kind of a test, too.

"Anything you need, you have it," Lexam said and closed the book, putting it under his arm. Rex nodded. "Thank you," he replied as he turned and walked right back towards the elevator. He stepped inside and at once the water drained out. Rex coughed, getting back to breathing air a great as warm wind flooded the small chamber and he dried out immediately.

He stepped back into the chamber that was still filled with chaos, Bonnie met him at the door.

"Assemble the crew, apparently, we have a black unicorn to find," Rex said to her quietly and her eyes went wide. "You really think one exists?" she asked him and Rex shook his head. "It really doesn't matter what I think, the King thinks it's real so that's good enough for me," Rex replied to her and had no idea what he would end up finding, or even where to look first. "Alright, I'll assemble the rest of the crew," Bonnie replied and walked away.

But first thing was first. He had to make a phone call to his wife, just in case any of this was real. He reached in his pocket and pulled out his own phone, pressed one button and waited.

"Hey. It's me," he said with a smile. "Yeah, you too, listen, the word is that there could be a Black Unicorn out there somewhere. The king seems to think so and I am going to investigate this. Do you think you could stay with your sister in the Southern Kingdom for a few days, just to be safe?" Rex asked with a smile.

"Yeah I know it's all just a big story but just on the off chance that there might be something to it, it's be better to be safe rather than sorry," Rex said and sighed. "Well, you can do it if you want to but if the thing is real don't say I didn't warn you," he said and continued, "love you, it's time for me to get back to work. I will talk to you later," Rex said and hung up the phone, put it back in his pocket. He turned back to the chaos of the command center and couldn't wait to get out of here.

"Alright everyone listen up," Rex shouted over the noise and the chaos died down. "The King thinks this is a black unicorn situation. Now, personally I don't believe any of it but we do have a town out there that was wiped off the map. I want the Voltarice prepped in twenty minutes, it's going to be a long day for all of us so everyone get organized and be ready for anything," Rex said to the people and the chaos finally started to make some amount of sense as they had some direction to follow.

Chapter 3

Nymie was passed out on her bed, snoring away from a late night of watching old monster movies and snacking on chocolate bars. It was her month off and she had earned it after saving a small undersea village from a Cryo horn attack. Her phone rang and she ignored it, anyone calling would call back later. She didn't care about anything and only wanted to go back to dreams. Suddenly her phone answered itself.

"Nymie, are you awake, it's me Rex. We have a situation," she groaned and turned over, putting a pillow over her head. "No, seriously I can hear you groaning over there, wake up, we have a potential black unicorn situation on our hands and this is obviously an all personnel on deck situation. I need you to wake up," Rex said to her. The words black unicorn shot through her dreams as if they were a bullet and she was immediately wide awake.

"Black unicorns aren't real. Why are you pranking me on my month off, Rex?" she demanded to know. "No prank Nymie, this is the real thing. Maybe. Lexam wants it investigated, be here as soon as you can," Rex said and the phone hung up.

Nymie sat up and her back cracked as she did so. "Trolls weren't meant to get up this early," she said. The idea of a black unicorn was stupid and she didn't know what was going on. She turned on the news to catch the tail end of a developing story. "We'll have more on the attack on Larenville after this break," the reporter said and it all went to a commercial that she didn't pay attention too. She'd never heard of that place but a feeling in her stomach told her that the phone call she got had something to do with this.

It was hard to believe a stupid trial of some royal dishwasher from the Northern Kingdom was over riding all but the worst stories this world had to offer. Not too many people cared about some village outside of the sea wall since everything almost came to an end, or appeared to. Nymie slowly stood up and shuffled her way into the bathroom to take a shower and get ready for work, even if it was her month off the call of duty was never one to be ignored.

"Am I going to die, doc?" a worried dwarf sat on the edge of a bed, sniffling. "For the third time, no, but you might want to get that mental problem you have checked out, it's just a cold, man. Go home and drink water, sleep for days and you'll be fine," Boz said and started filling out a prescription for some kind of generic pain killers. "Are you sure doc, I mean my aunt had a cold just like this and a week later she was dead, dead you hear me?" the dwarf asked. Boz stopped writing.

"A week later you say? Well, sounds to me like it was more of a plague mage's curse, but I did a magic scan on you remember, no curses," Boz said with a smile and he finished writing, ripped of the note pad and handed it to him. "Give this to the nice lady behind the counter and be sure not to sneeze on her, okay," Boz said and the man took the paper, stood up and walked out without saying a single word.

"You're welcome you paranoid nutjob," Boz said after the doors closed and took his latex gloves off when his phone began to ring. He answered it, "Yeah, what is it," he said, annoyed at the last patient and walked out of his office so the cleansing charms could work.

"You bet I'm ready to get out of this hellhole," Boz replied. "A black unicorn, you're kidding," Boz said as he brushed his golden hair behind his pointed elf ears. It sounds like a good hunt and money for nothing but sure, I'm up for it," he said and smiled.

"Meet you soon," he said and hung up the phone. The medical officer took off his white overcoat and tossed it over the chair. He pushed a button on the wall and the microphone clicked. "Sarah, call in Dr. Norb. I've been called away on royal business," he said into it. "Will do, thanks for the notice this time, doctor," she replied and he smiled. "Yeah, sorry. I'm forgetful about the little things like telling people where I am going, it's a problem," he replied and let the button go. He took off his long white overcoat and hung it on a nearby doorknob.

He took one last look around and walked out the door. Boz was a little excited, he'd always believed in the possibility of the black unicorn existing, but at the same time a little afraid of it.

Evie was meditating in her underwater chamber before an image of Elrox, the god of the sea and the creator of all her kind. She had been sitting cross legged in the middle of her room for hours thinking about nothing, trying to channel the Ethereal ocean. She was wearing nothing but a thin, see through ceremonial robe exposing her smooth, green interlocking scales of her body. Then the statue began to speak to her.

"Evie, answer the phone," it said in a soft whisper and continued, "You will be needed for what comes next," the statue finished and Evie jumped out of her position, only to immediately float back to the ground. The statue had never done anything before let alone spoke, but as she looked at it now there was nothing different about it. Sure, enough the phone rang and she picked it up.

"Hello?" she asked.

"I was expecting you, I'll explain later," she said into the phone and never took her eyes off that statue. "I'll be at the castle as soon as I am dressed," she said and hung up before Rex could even say goodbye.

"Not sure what you think I can do, Elrox, but I will do my best to do what you're expecting me to do, or, you know, try," Evie said, the Elroxian mage swam upright in a second. "Zolt," she said and at once her thin robe turned into a much thicker green robe to match her green scales, it was thick and flowed in the water weightlessly. An emerald staff appeared in her hands and she smiled, spun it around in her hands. A bright blue shaft of light appeared around her, then she was gone leaving nothing but a column of bubbles behind in her wake.

The sun was over the horizon, just long enough for Tayne to close the black shades to block the light out. Tayne was relocated from the Morglands to serve as a unicorn hunter. Tayne's work dove into the deeper, worse part of hunting. There were types of unicorns out there living beings should never come near, and this is what he was good at. Tayne lay down in his bed, shifted just enough to get comfortable and close his deep red eyes when the phone rang.

"Son of a snozbucket who the hell is calling me," he said, reached over for his phone and pulled it to him. "Damn it, what do you want," he growled and answered it. "Black unicorns aren't real, you're drunk on something, go home," Tayne growled back to him and almost hung up. "You know, I don't care if the world is coming to an end, I had a long night. A pair of blood horns were hunting just outside of Nyrn last night. Three kids were taken and I, well, I lost them. The unicorns are banished but I was too late I need a break," Tayne said, not one to hold back on some of the things he had seen, "I'm tired," he finished saying.

"What do you mean Lexam wants everyone on board, we don't work together. Who's going to patrol if we are all out on a wild goose chase. This feels like a trap to me. Doesn't it feel weird to you to call in all the top people to just one spot?" Tayne asked, he was tired but not stupid. This was less to do with being objective and just not wanting to go out in the daylight even more.

"Fine, Bonnie, you don't need to start barking out the royal orders, I'll go if I have too," he said and groaned about it. Vampires didn't need to sleep but the sunlight drained their strength and energy to the point that sleeping was a great option. He hung up the phone, threw off the covers and sat up again. "Xy, don't let the sunburn be too bad, that's all I ask," he said a little prayer as he stood up and made his way to his refrigerator and opened it. There was no light on the inside.

He pulled out a large glass bottle of human blood, opened it and drank half of it in one shot. He wiped off the residue on his mouth and the blood reenergized him immediately. He closed the bottle and put it back into the fridge. He walked to his closet and got dressed.

All it was this time however was a pair of black jeans and a t-shirt to match. He slipped on his shoes, sunglasses, and grabbed his keys. Tayne opened the door and winced at the intensity of the sun. "Daylight is so overrated," he said and quickly made his way to his car and got in.

He started it and switched the windows to daylight mode. Immediately they filtered out most of the sunlight rendering the outsides completely black. Black windows were illegal on cars except for those considered undead, or in the Morglands. If any guard pulled him over he'd be sure to give them a piece of his mind.

Drask was spending her morning watching the news, drinking hot rum and soaking her feet in hot water that was near boiling wrapped in a light blanket and nothing else. She was in heaven as far as most dwarves were concerned. Being a unicorn hunter was tough work but it was very rewarding and she used her money well to live the best she could.

"Come on, we all know that Kenders opened up the blade, convict the little twerp and get it over already," she shouted at the television but had no urge to do much more than that. She set her rum down and picked up her pipe put it between her lips and inhaled a large amount of smoke. It made her feel better. It was a long night as a Diamond horn clawed its way out of the ground and decided to terrorize a small town. She just got home only two hours before the sunrise and she was relaxing the only way she knew how to do it.

Then the phone rang.

"Damn it, what in the seven hells is this about, why is my phone ringing," she glared at it, angrily. Took another puff of the pipe to try to calm down then answered the phone. "Yeah, what do you want," she said in one breath and narrowed her eyes, the commercial for some new pill they made was just about over and the trial was going to be back on and she wanted to see it play out.

"No, I just got home, everything hurts so I need to recover. I'm not a machine or a vampire. I have limits," she replied as the commercial came to an end. "You don't even know anything about a black unicorn, nobody does besides one small line of ancient nonsense, it's not even a thing," Drask replied, not buying any of it.

"Lexam can go screw himself and his waterlogged throne, I'm not going anywhere," she yelled again as her show came back on.

"What do you mean its mandatory?" she asked him and put the pipe down. "Fine, but I'm not driving. Send a car out for me, no, a limo. Bring a limo. I need to sleep on the way there, I've been up for about two days fighting a diamond horn. It's banished, no worries, I'll be ready but you better be on time," she said and pushed the button to hang up. "I'll guess I'll never know if you did it, but I know you did it," Drask said and narrowed her golden eyes at the television. She stood up and her body rebelled as her bones cracked into place and muscles strained. She stepped out of the cooling water as the blanket around her fell off around her on to her chair. She slowly walked to her bedroom threw open her closet and began pulling out things to wear.

In her tired state of mind nothing was quite making sense anymore. She threw on an old green t-shirt and a pair of blue jeans. Neither one fit quite right, the pants were too tight and the shirt was too big.

"I'll have Evie fix it later, who cares," she said and stumbled out of the room and straight into her front porch. "Lights off, please," she said and not only all the lights went off, but the television too.

She sat in her rocking chair, pulled her golden brown hair back out of her face and leaned back into the chair. "Any time now," she said and looked off into the sun shining through the mist, she saw a black limo coming in her direction. "I have to figure out how they get around so quick," Drask said, fighting off the latest urge to pass out before they arrived.

"I called all the top ranked hunters and they all, well, they all agreed to show up for this," she said and Rex looked at her. "Agreed, you practically told them not showing up would be considered treason, you really think that any of them would have said no?" Rex replied to her. "Well sometimes you need to do whatever it takes to get your way. If this is real enough to get the King all worked up about it, we are obligated to investigate it with all hands on deck don't you think," she said and Rex just shrugged. "It'll be the easiest money we ever made," he replied then changed the subject.

"Let's go see Voltarice," he said, changing the subject and Bonnie just shook her head. "It's been awhile since she's been up and running we've taken care of her, you'll see," Bonnie replied and the two of them walked away from the chaotic command center back to the elevator.

"Keep the star, Rex, you may need it in the future," Bonnie said to him as the doors opened and they stepped in. "Well thanks for that, I'll keep it safe I promise," he said and the doors closed around them.

The trip wasn't very long and due to the magical nature of the elevator, down or up wasn't exactly a direction they could tell they were going. Minutes later the doors opened and the two of them stepped out in to the docking bay.

Chapter 4

Before them the great airship Voltarice sat there in silence, it was just as he remembered it being. A massive silver airship that was designed to do this job. "It's a thing of beauty isn't it?" Evie asked, already there in the loading bay, waiting for them in her green robe. Rex jumped at her voice, he didn't see her there.

"Yeah it is, how did you get around the wards?" Rex asked her and she smiled. "I helped ward the place, remember, I know a few things. Teleportation spells are great thing," she replied.

Rex still didn't look at her. "The others will be here soon, you might as well get on the ship and start getting ready to leave," Rex said and turned around only to see a fading blue light. "Oh," he said to himself and sighed.

"Mages are so hard to talk to sometimes," he said and started to walk towards the ship. "Bonnie, go back to the command center and make sure that there isn't anyone trying to start anything on fire, alright. We'll need you there. Keep a lid on this from the media until you hear from me. I am sure some nosy reporters have already beaten us to the punch but contact the networks. Tell them it's more air time they can dedicate to that stupid trial, it should work," Rex said, Bonnie nodded. "Yeah, I'll see if I can't get Lexam on the blackout, too," she said and walked back towards the elevator.

"Alright ship, let's see if I still remember how to run you," he said to no one and walked towards the thing. Voltarice scanned him at once with a blue beam and immediately Rex was transported onto the ship. "Welcome aboard, Commander," a voice said to him and he smiled, no one had called him that in a while but he didn't mind.

"Thank you, Voltarice, could you give me a status report, please," he asked as he walked towards the bridge. "We are ready to go any time you wish, everything is one hundred percent," the computer voice said to him and he smiled. "Perfect, as soon as the rest of them get here we can leave," he said and kept walking down the white halls. "Understood, Commander," she replied and went silent.

One by one the rest of the crew began to arrive. It was only about an hour after the last phone call. Rex watched them all show up as he sat in the chair and couldn't help but laugh at himself. These people rarely worked together unless their districts over lapped.

They didn't get along and if there was anyone else he could have called he would have done just that, but these were the top ranked unicorn hunters in the Western Kingdom and he needed them now. He could only hope that it was all for nothing in the end and everything he was confronted with right now was nothing more than and a false alarm and an easy paycheck for all of them.

Rex got out of his chair and started to make his way towards the teleportation room. He knew they would all come aboard at the same time. No one liked being first in this group, except for Evie, but she liked to stay in her water filled chamber.

Not that he blamed her for that, being an Elroxian on an airship was marginally difficult at the best of times.

Rex stood outside of the chamber. "Four crew members teleporting now," the ship said to him and a blue light flashed, they were all standing there before him. "Hi guys, how's it going?" Rex tried to lighten the mood but none of them were happy to see him really.

"Shove off, little man," Nymie said to him and stormed past him, Drask said nothing, too tired to talk and followed her. "Hey, Rex, I'm glad to see you at least," Boz said and reached out to shake his hand. Rex returned the gesture and was happy at least someone was in a positive mood.

Tayne glared at Rex and cracked his neck. "Are all the supplies on this can yet? I'm thirsty and don't want to eat one of the scrubs that are running around here," he said and Boz looked at him. "I could give you a bloodpatch you know, it could help you, Tayne," Boz said and looked at him. "Yeah, but I've seen plenty of vampires get addicted to those things and go really bad. I think I'll just stick to the old-fashioned thing, but thanks anyway," Tayne replied and Rex interjected.

"Yeah, the supplies are on board. I have your quarters stocked with all the blood you could ever need, just make sure you don't ask where it came from. I know you like the human stuff but we got some from everyone," Rex said and both Boz and Tayne shuddered at the thought.

"I guess it'll have to do, thanks," Tayne said and started to walk down towards his quarters. "Don't worry Boz, the sick bay is equipped too. I hope we won't need it, or you, don't take it personal," Rex said to him. "Honestly I hope you don't need me either. I don't want to put any of you back together, so let's stay safe out there alright," Boz replied and started to walk down to the sick bay. Rex smiled, but he knew that Boz really wanted to play the heroic medic type so he could brag about it at some point to show off.

"Great, my crew leaders are all overly tired and cranky. I guess I can do auto pilot," he said to himself and began to make his way back to the bridge by himself.

"Voltarice, start the engines, we are leaving," he said to the ship and there was a great shudder as the engines came to life. "Yes, sir," the computer replied.

Rex got to the bridge and turned on the intercom.

"This is your Commander speaking, our destination is thirty miles outside the wall, we will have three hours before we get to the wall so use this time now to get some sleep, eat, rest, do whatever. Once we get there it's all hands on deck, so enjoy the off time while you can," Rex said into the intercom and shut it off. Rex sat in the helm control station.

"Alright, help me take us out as easy as it goes," he said to the ship. The Voltarice rose into the air of the ground and the docking door opened. Slowly the silver ship exited the castle docking bay and rose into the misty air. Rex was nervous, the last thing he wanted to do was scrape the side of the castle with everyone watching, including the King. Thankfully for him he was able to maneuver the thousand foot long ship out of the way of any danger.

"Good deal, Voltarice, set a course to sector twenty three on the wall, tell me once we get there and I'll take it from there," he said to the ship. "Yes, sir," the voice responded to him. Now all that was left was the waiting, at least for now.

The trip took almost as long as Rex said it would, all was quiet on the ship.

"All senior officers report to the bridge," Rex's voice came over the intercom. The still worn out crew forced themselves to the bridge one at a time. Rex was waiting for them to show up already. Evie was the first one in the door and looked out the viewing window.

"Look at that wall, legend says that Elrox built it in one day from the bones of massive sea dragons that threatened to drown the world," Evie said and stared at the massive thing in the screen.

"I don't know about legends but I do know it spreads out for thousands of miles protecting the outer edge of the Western Kingdom," Rex said, neither of them saw the wall very often but it was always awe inspiring. The others came through the door on at a time.

"Haven't been out here since my training days," Nymie said as she the saw it. "Ditto," Drask said but Boz wasn't impressed. "On my off time I come out here all the time because doctors aren't common out here. It's a living," he said, trying to one up all of them, but he didn't get a response.

Tayne crossed his arms, but didn't have a comment.

Before them was a great wall of shining, sparkling green stone that stretched out from left to right as far as the eye could see, and nothing else but the blue green waters of the Yalo ocean on the other side of it.

"Beyond the wall are the wild, untamed ocean lands. I'm not sure why anyone would want to live way out there," Tayne said as the ship flew over the wall.

"Hello Voltarice, nice to see you out this way again. Good luck over the wall, we'll wait for your return," a voice said through their speakers and continued, "This is the Emerald Watch, signing out," the voice said and the speakers went dead.

"I guess that's their way of telling us goodbye," Drask said as she gazed into the endless ocean beyond the wall. "We're all nervous, don't worry about a thing, I think we'll be fine," Rex replied.

In just a few minutes the Voltarice had cleared the wall and flew out to open water.

"Drask, Tayne, enough standing around, get to your stations, Boz keep an eye on our surroundings and let me know if anything is about to eat us, you're the science officer now, I guess," Rex said and looked at Evie. "You make sure nothing is watching us. If you sense anything, and I mean anything, let me know," he said and was relying on her the most here, magic could sense things sensors couldn't and there were plenty of nasty things out here.

"So, I have to know something," Drask said to Rex and continued, "How does it burn anything underwater, why was there a Pyro here, at all. None of this makes any sense," she asked and Rex shrugged. "There is only one way I can think of this could have worked if it was a Pyro, but it still seems very much impossible. Listen, let's not speculate too much, let's do it like any other thing and work with the evidence we find," Rex replied. Drask just nodded.

"All stations, prepare to dive in five minutes," Rex said at once through the intercom and waited for all stations to report green. One by one all the lights on his panel began to turn green. It only took three minutes before all stations reported to be ready.

"Well, they work fast," Rex said to himself, flipped the intercom switch. "Diving now, please report any leaks if you see them, thank you," Rex said and shut the thing off.

The thousand foot ship stopped in midair and slowly sank to the surface of the sea, then the silver metal giant slowly disappeared under the waves with barely enough force to disturb the ocean. Within seconds it was as if it was never there at all.

Chapter 5

Despite the darkness of the water, no one detected any amount of danger around them. "Are you sure there is a monster down here?" Tayne asked and stared at the radar, bored out of his mind already. "I am sure there are lots of monsters down here, but most of them aren't dumb enough to attack a ship this big, don't worry we'll be fine until we get there," Rex replied and resisted the urge to roll his eyes.

The rest of the short trip to the crime scene was easy.

"Well, will you look at that," Drask said as they saw the village on the bottom of the ocean, surrounded by a massive shield.

"Very weird, the outer villages only turn their shields on for about three months to get supplies they can't make on their own during the calm weather," Boz said and immediately knew there was something of a problem going on down there right away. "How weird is it really? The Emerald Watch got here before we did, use your head," Drask replied.

"Oh, well, yeah it could be them too, I guess," Boz replied as he was embarrassed by Drask.

"Get us into teleporting range we're all going down there so be ready," Rex said and stood up, he hated sitting too long in one spot because it made him restless. "So many damned questions, none of this makes any sense," Nymie said what most of them were thinking.

Drask just wanted another mug of hot rum and to get back to sleeping. If there was a rogue Pyrohorn down there, it was going to pay for ruining her time off.

Voltarice made it into teleportation range and floated above the village.

"If you need a weapon you know where the armory is, choose your weapon wisely, because there is no telling what could be down there and grab an Aquarian Star too while you're at it," Rex said and continued, "whatever weapon you pick make sure it can work underwater if need be," he finished and turned to walk out of the bridge.

"Zola, you have the bridge," he said and she looked at him in surprise. The officer shot to unexpected attention, and surprise as her black eyes widened.

"But I, I mean yes sir," she replied. She had only run the ship in simulations before and had no intention to actually run the thing at any capacity. Rex nodded with a smile. "Don't worry, the worst you can do is blow the thing up and kill everyone, I think you'll be fine," Rex said before he left the bridge.

She swallowed nervously in response, then was determined to do the best she could.

Zola felt there was no need to worry the rest of the crew over a maybe, however so she kept it to herself. The senior hunters quickly put their stations into auto pilot and locked them into place before getting up and leaving the bridge one by one, she made her way to the Commander's chair and sat down. The rest of the crew looked at her.

"We'll be fine, monitor the situation and start scanning the village for anything, I don't know, weird," she ordered and the rest of the crew got to work.

"This is your Commander speaking, the senior officers are going to be going to the surface, until then Lt Zola is going to be in charge, listen to her as you would me," Rex said into the intercom from the transporter room, waiting for the others. An Elroxian crewman was manning the teleportation console.

"Sir, do you think that Zola can be trusted," he asked Rex.

Rex turned to the man and glared at him. "I have to trust someone, and until I have reason to otherwise we will continue to do so," he replied and the crewman felt scared for speaking like he did out of turn as soon as Rex finished, but the Commander let it go and stepped on to the transporter without saying another word.

"The others will be here soon," he said and wondered what was taking them so long.

The others were in the Armory of the ship and they were all deciding on what weapons to pick. Boz wasn't a fan of weapons, he picked up an electric blade and swung it around a couple of times for no reason other than to see that it wouldn't fall apart mid swing.

"Evie, could you waterproof my blade for me," he asked her and she smiled at him. "Yeah, I can do that but wouldn't a bow and arrow be better for you, elf?" she asked with a smile and Boz cast a narrow eyed glance in her direction. "How much more racist can you get?" he asked and she smiled.

"Kidding old man, Cheltax," she said and a flash of purple light covered his electric sword for a brief moment. "There it's proofed for about fifteen hours, that should be more than enough time," Evie said and repeated the spell for all the weapons, just in case it was needed.

"There, how hurry up and pick something," she said to them. Tayne reached on the rack and picked up a combat shotgun with a magical ammo chamber. Drask picked up a plasma rifle. Nymie picked up an enchanted battle axe and placed it against her back, the enchantment held it in place. Each of them picked up an Aquarian crest that was hanging on the wall beside them and hung it around their necks.

"Alright, let's go see what this black unicorn nonsense is all about so we can all go back home," Drask said to them and they all agreed with that. The five of them made their way back to the teleporting room where Rex was waiting.

"What took you guys so long I was about to take a nap," Rex said to them and they just scowled back in response.

"Alright, damn, it isn't like I accused you of treason or anything," Rex said as they all stepped on to the platform. "No, but you are the only one who seems to be in a good mood about any of this," Drask replied and Rex just smiled. "I just have to remain positive as much as I can, negativity is infectious," he replied, it was true, too.

"At best a pyre horn did attack and wipe this place out, at worse we have to find a way to deal with a mythical beast no one has ever seen, it's not a good day either way you look at it," Boz replied to him. Rex decided that the time for small talk was over.

"Energize," Rex said to the operator. In seconds they were all gone in a blue light.

"I will need as many ash samples as you can get out of section A through F, I think that is where the attack started," Chief Moreno said to an Elroxian in a bright orange hazmat suit. "I'll get a team on it right away," the agent responded and shuffled away. Then the blue light cut into the air behind him and he turned around, never noticing the massive ship above the village due to how dark the water was above him.

"What the hell took you guys so long?" Moreno asked them. "We got here as fast as we could, what do we know?" Rex asked and got right to the point. "Pyrehorn blasted through here just before sunrise. The ash is spread out starting over here. People ran, it blasted, you know the rest. The ash isn't telling us much but then again, we aren't experts. You may want to wear a mask down here, without circulation the ash will shred your lungs," Moreno replied.

"We don't plan on being here that long," Tayne replied.

"Unicorns are what we deal with, we're experts in the field, we'll be fine," Evie said and stepped forward.

"Yeah, if we work together we can figure this out a lot sooner than you think, I'll bet," Drask said to the chief. The man in the uniform looked away, he wanted to say more but at the same time needed to keep it professional with people like these.

"Alright spread out and see what you can find, report back to me with anything. Oh by the way, this place has a name. It, well it used to be Naber. Now it's just a ghost town," Moreno said to them and continued, "Also, we are pretty sure the beast is still here somewhere, when we got here, the shield was already up. There hasn't been any sign of the thing, but you know they can suppress their fire when needed," he finished and walked away from them.

"Alright team, figure out what happened here, if you find the beast, banish it. You are all capable of doing it on your own," Rex said and they all agreed on that with a silent nod. They all knew the stakes. An entire village of people had been wiped out. It was easy to get angry, however they all suppressed those feelings. One moment of distraction could have meant death. They all went their separate ways to find information.

Chapter 6

Boz immediately stopped when a drip of water hit his hand and he looked up.

"Shields don't usually leak," he said but didn't see where the water could have come from. He walked towards the center of Naber and found what he was looking for. The rest of the crime scene investigators were too busy collecting ashes and looking for clues that no one was bothering to look at the shield tower generator. He had been to enough of these small villages to know they all had one and how they worked. He walked up to it and opened the maintenance panel, there was a computer screen to greet him.

"These are the worst investigators ever," Boz said to himself and started to punch in keys to get a status read out, it was all he could do without the access codes to get deeper into the system.

"Hours ago, the shield was turned on at half strength by user twenty three for a routine test of the shield crystal matrix," a quiet voice said to him.

Boz typed in the screen, *who is user twenty-three?*

"User unknown to system," the voice replied and Boz scoffed at the inconvenience. "A shield at half strength would have let water through, it would have looked just like, or been similar to rain for as long as it was half power," he looked up and wondered why anyone would do something like that.

A man in a hazmat suit walked up to him. "We already checked this, user number twenty three doesn't have a name. The shield was still at half strength when we got here, it was how we got in to this place, we're working here mister Elf, don't be so harsh," he said to Boz, but the elf was not fazed. "Next time just ask," the man in the suit said and Boz narrowed his eyes at the screen he was looking at.

"You might be a member of the Emerald Watch, but make no mistake, talk to me like that again and I will make you regret it," Boz said with a deeper voice. The man behind him took a step back.

"But you raise a good point to ask anyway, but still if we can access the system we can find out what happened. These towers often act as silent guardians, watching everything, it's a little secret they use to keep crime at a minimum out here. If you have a Tech guy send him my way so we can get to the bottom of this?" Boz half asked and more demanded and the hazmat man seemed shocked by this information.

"Yes sir, right away," he replied and shuffled off noisily. "Rookies," Boz said as he walked away from the tower, waiting for someone to show up.

Drask walked down mud path and made her way into the local bar that was called The Golden Fish. It was one of the most primitive places she'd ever seen. Everything was made out of stone and coral. This place was made to exist and function underwater so it made sense but it was nowhere near comfortable to her.

But she moved right up to the counter and around it. There was a black bottle of Deloid Rum, common drink of the Elroxians and it was unopened under the bar. Oddly, it was the only bottle left in the place. "Weird," she said to herself.

She picked it up and twisted the cap off to take a big swig of it. The liquid immediately burned her throat and she winced, placed the bottle back on the counter. "We'll just pretend that never happened," she said and looked around, the burn fading away just as fast as it came.

Oddly enough there were no burned shadows on the wall here. Well, she just figured that this attack happened after the place closed.

She decided to check the place out a little more and walked into the back where the dish room was. She figured doing dishes underwater must have been pretty easy, but when she walked in the light turned on and there she found a dead body with two black knives through the eyes of the victim and their chest was carved open. All of their insides were removed and inside was filled with broken glass.

"Oh, what fresh hell is this," she said and immediately took a step back, picked up her communicator. "Rex, I have a victim that looks like he's been ritually sacrificed, it's a scene right out of a movie in here. I'm at the Golden Fish, you need to see this, bring a couple of those investigators, too," she said into it and all she could do is stare at the victim.

"I'm on my way," Rex replied.

At least now she knew where all the other bottles went too. With any luck, there would be fingerprints on some of the glass shards to give them more clues. One thing was for sure, a unicorn didn't do this.

Tayne wasn't very impressed with what he was seeing so far but didn't mind the whole no sun thing down here. If the constant exposure to the water didn't have such a terrible effect on the undead like himself, he would have lived here himself. He grabbed an Aquarian star for the extra protection from the element.

This place was dark in more than one way, besides the investigators there wasn't any signs of life. No pets, no people, nothing. The place was almost completely sterile, even the weak life force of bacteria could barely be detected. What kind of flame only burned flesh to ash, but left the buildings standing?

Tayne worried because he'd never seen anything like this before. He walked down the muddy path and stopped when he felt that something was standing there behind him. It was less something he knew and more of a suspicion.

He turned around and standing there was a machine woman that had clearly been burned. Half of its skin was melted off and the silver steel was blackened. "Help me," it said and started to walk towards him. "Okay, what happened here. I can't help you until I know what happened," Tayne said and tried to get some information out of it. "Help me," the machine said again and started to walk faster.

"Oh, so you're broken beyond repair and were turned into a killing machine, great," Tayne said to himself and got ready for a fight. The metal woman took a clumsy swing with its left, exposed metal fist. "No," Tayne said, stepped out of the way and watched the machine fall to the ground. "Help me," it said again as it began to struggle to get back up. Tayne saw something on the back of its metal skull that didn't belong. He put his foot on her back, pressed her to the ground with ease.

Tayne bent over and pulled the red chip off of her metal skull, her body went limp. Tayne stood back up and investigated it. "Second rate remote control device," he said, knowing what it was but that was about it. The machine did nothing for a second, then it jerked to life.

"What happened, where am I?" she asked and Tayne took his foot off her back. "That's what I am trying to figure out," he replied to her as she pulled herself out of the mud. "I appear to be damaged," she said to mostly herself and looked down and continued. "I am sorry for my appearance," she said and Tayne didn't care one way or another.

"Don't sweat it you're fine. What's the last thing you remember?" he said still inspecting the red controller chip. "I was testing the shield to make sure it worked, we do it once a month. This is my routine, I am number twenty three. This is what I do," she said trying to wipe the mud off as much as she could and trying to look presentable.

"Well I have some bad news. At some point after you did that you were attacked by a Pyrehorn and someone used you to let it in. Everyone you know has been, well, vaporized, I'm sorry," he said and she bowed her burned, half metal head in sadness. Tayne didn't think too many machines felt that many emotions or anything really.

"I was the utility bot, they called me Unie. I fixed things. I made sure everything was running," she said and trailed off. "How did you exist down here, you're, um a machine," Tayne said as he put the red chip down and put it in his pocket. "I'm enchanted to resist the water, any other stupid questions or will you tell where I can find a place to repair myself?" she asked and Tayne shook his head.

"I don't know, unless you have a repair bay in town we only have the ship, and no one gets on the ship without clearance. Let's go see Rex and see what we can do for you," he said and the two of them began walk towards the center of Naber when his radio came to life with the grim details of Drask's find.

"Well damn, that sucks. We better go see the unspeakable scene of tragic horror, sounds like fun, right?" Tayne said and the machine just looked at him. "No, it does not," Unie replied to him and the two began to walk towards the bar.

Nymie didn't go too far from the teleportation site and there on a long wall of some building. She had no idea what it was for but all along the grey walls were black markings in the shape of people with their hands up of varying heights, obviously some of them were children.

"Creepy sight isn't it?" someone in a hazmat suit asked as they walked up to her. "I'll never get used to it, I've just never seen so many in one place like this before," she said not taking her eyes off of the scene. "I don't think too many have, not since the old days anyway," he said and Nymie remembered reading about the Southern Kingdom's problems before the unicorn hunters were an official thing. Reports of entire towns being blasted into ashes overnight were surprisingly common and horrific.

"Well, we need to find out how this happened. I mean, it makes no sense that one of them would be all the way under the ocean like this," she replied and the person in the suit nodded. "We can't figure it out either, nor can we figure out how it even got here. The attack started on the eastern side of town and the thing quickly incinerated anyone who tried to escape, but then there is this wall. It's as if they all stood here waiting to die. Normal people don't do that. Someone had to be holding them here. Have you ever heard of someone controlling a unicorn before? We think someone found a way to do it," they said to her and Nymie was confused about all of this and had never even thought that was possible.

"If someone found a way to control a unicorn they are literally playing with fire. I'm sure that a thing like that doesn't appreciate being on a leash, I know I sure don't like it," she said quietly. "What was that?" he asked quickly. She caught what she said and shook her head. "Nothing, nothing, show me where this attack started," she said and changed the subject.

It was about then the details if the Dwarf's find came over her radio. Nymie wanted to see the origin of the attack but figured this was more important.

"Hey, why are you all in these getups anyway? There doesn't seem to be anything wrong with this place besides the lack of people," she said looking around. "Initial scans reported a large amount of radiation when we got here, that and all the ash in the air," he said and started to walk away.

"Oh, well we didn't detect anything like that. The ship would have warned us about that before we came down here," she said, but when she looked around saw that she was alone. "Right then, I'm gonna go this way," she continued to say and walked towards the bar, she could see the sign from where she was.

"Figures Drask would find the remains at a bar and make her way there first thing. I'll be sure to not mention that when I get there," she said to herself as walked in that direction.

Chapter 7

The four of them met up at the door of the bar and Drask was there to meet them in a chair she pulled out from the inside. "You guys can go in, I don't need to see that again," she said to them and took another drink out of her black bottle. "It's ritualistic and I don't know what it means," she added and shook her head. "There are a number of cults that worship the beast and, hey, who is that?" Nymie asked as she noticed the burned machine woman behind Tayne.

"Utility bot, she was being controlled by some red chip thing on her head. I, like the total amazing hero I am, saved her," he said with a blank stare.

"Right," she replied and Rex decided to take the lead.

"Alright, we will deal with the robot girl later. see what this is all about for now. Tayne, you're with me the rest of you stay out here and watch for, well, anything weird," Rex said and Nymie looked around. "I see all kinds of weird things, when do we start warning people?" she asked and Rex rolled his eyes. "Aggressive, okay, anything aggressive or a rampaging, burning unicorn," Rex said and couldn't believe he had to clarify that. Nymie just smiled. "I'm just messing with you, get inside already," she replied and turned her eyes back to the empty village, waiting for anything horrible.

"If it's a magic thing, shouldn't I come with, too?" Evie asked and Rex just shrugged. "It's a small space, you're right outside if we need you, be ready," Rex replied to her and nodded to Tayne.

Tayne and Rex walked into the bar and moved towards the back. "I knew Elroxians liked their places simple but this is nearly primitive," Rex said. "Yeah, it might be a thousand years old. It doesn't look like much but these people build things to last.

They entered the dish room and saw nothing.

"Uh, what the hell is going on," Rex said as immediately he looked around, and the place was clean, well as a dish room could be expected to be. "No, look there near the wall," Tayne pointed and there was a piece of black glass there on the floor.

"Two options. The dead thing got up and walked out, or something took the body out and she didn't notice either way who or whatever caused this attack is still out here. It's screwing with us," Rex said and walked over, picked up the glass piece. It was just a typical piece of a bottle. Tayne looked up, expecting to see something horrible there looking back at him on the ceiling.

There was nothing there and he was relieved only slightly.

"Well, I guess we better go tell her that there wasn't anyone in there, but she's not insane. If she saw something I believe her," Rex said with a sigh. "Did you see that bottle in her hand? She's drinking already and we don't know what that stuff is. She could be seeing things. There might not be anything here or ever was," Tayne said and Rex nodded.

"True, but we need to assume everything right now. I've never seen anything like she described," Rex said, trying to think of what it might have meant. "I'll have Evie to take a look around, too and Drask can scan the place to see if there is anything in there," Rex replied to him taking one last look around the place but seeing nothing out of the ordinary.

Anyway, let's get out of here, this place is giving me the creeps," Tayne said and couldn't explain why it was.

The two of them walked out of the bar and back to the others who was waiting for the news. "The place is empty, no body, not even any blood in the room. All we found was this one, tiny piece of glass," Rex held it up for everyone to see. Evie was about to talk, so was Boz when Drask erupted in frustration.

"Son of a squorb, no, that's not what I saw, that's not possible. I saw the whole scene. That's impossible," Drask said and tried to take another swig of the bottle when a metal hand wrapped around her wrist. "I do not know what you are drinking, but this can't be good for you in a situation like this," she said to her and quickly took the bottle away from her, smashing it to the ground.

Drask stood up and grabbed the machine by the throat. "I'll take you apart if you touch me again, robot," she said and was strong enough to escape the machines grasp but just barely. After she was free she rubbed her wrist and pushed herself away from the machine.

In the chaos, none of them saw the figure walking toward them.

"Unie is right, you know. One shouldn't drink on the job. That is just so wrong," a voice said to them that was unsettling and broken.

The group's troubles came to an end as they turned to face the stranger. He was an Elroxian that held long, black daggers in his hands and its stomach was melted together. Its eyes were gone and its scales were gray.

"What the hell are you supposed to be?" Rex asked, he really didn't care what it was. "I am the messenger, I see you got my message. I am pleased you got it. I was thinking that no one would. That would have made me, sad," the thing said, but the mouth and the words were delayed. The mouth kept moving after the words had finished.

Evie stepped forward, narrowed her eyes. "This is a poorly put together glass golem, or in other words just a puppet," she said but never broke eye contact with the thing. "Well then let's break it," Drask said and started to lift her weapon up.

"Who is the puppet master?" Tayne demanded to know and stepped forward, "What do you want from us?" he finished asked the thing. It tilted his head to the side as the question was asked and smiled.

"I needed you all here, in one place so I could, take care of the biggest threats I had to raising the Black Unicorn. The gods have returned, the true magic is back in place. The time is right to unleash the beast, I just don't need you getting in the way," it replied to them in a slow, deliberate fashion. The group was getting ready for anything. It obviously intended to kill them.

"Well that answers half the question, I guess," Rex said when suddenly there was a gunshot from down the road and the puppet was struck in the head from the right side, tiny shards of black glass sprayed into the mud but it didn't fall down. "That's the monster that did this, bring it down men," Moreno yelled and a small group of people with high powered rifles started shooting the thing. The five of them backed off at once to avoid any glass that might be coming their way.

Before the crew could do anything about it the poorly made golem was on the ground, nothing more than a lifeless suit of skin with black glass spilling out of the new wounds.

"Well thanks for saving us but, you know. I don't think that was needed. What was needed, was more information," Rex yelled to Moreno and the chief just shrugged in response.

"This thing was what made the attack happen, so I took care of it, problem solved," he replied. "No, you moron, that wasn't a person at all, it was a golem and–" Drask was cut off by a great orange light coming from down the opposite side of the street from the others. "Oh, well would you look at that," Drask said and shielded her eyes.

"I guess someone didn't like us breaking their toys, no chance the thing appears on its own just after mister glass here was broken," Nymie said to them.

"What? no one brings a unicorn anywhere," Rex replied as he drew his weapon. "Looks like the rules are changing. Someone figured out how to play a whole new game and now we need to learn what they are. Right now, we should take care of this little problem before we get fried," she replied as the burning thing took its first step towards them.

Despite being so far away they could all feel the heat that was coming off of it.

"Is that the monster who did this?" Moreno yelled out to the team. "No, that's the pizza delivery service's new gimmick that is going announce their arrival, what in the hell do you think man, what else would it be?" Rex yelled back but couldn't take his eyes off of it.

The beast, as terrifying as they usually were, this one was moving as if it were a machine. Every step was calculated, mechanical and forced. It escaped no one who could see it. "Okay so a unicorn is being controlled. This should make the job much easier,"

Evie said as she shielded her eyes from the intense firelight.

The flaming orange horn suddenly glowed bright blue and a stream of blue flame shot down the street. "Move," Rex yelled. Moreno got out of the way but five of his team didn't move quick enough. They were instantly incinerated, all that was left were their smoking feet as ashes floated down the street leaving the smell of melted plastic and charred flesh behind.

"Yeah, that would explain all the things, but it doesn't answer any of the questions," Nymie said as she watched the people evaporate before her eyes. "Great, let's not be the next ones to die, does that sound like a good plan to you?" Drask said as the monster turned its attention on to them.

"Perfect," Rex replied as they all scattered in different directions from the front of the bar. The beast fired again and the bar exploded on impact sending bright blue and white fire in all directions.

Chapter 8

Boz, still waiting for a tech specialist looked to his left just in time to see a high explosion of blue and white flames. "There are only a few things alive that makes fire like that," Boz said to himself. He looked around and saw the other people shuffling in their plastic suits from the explosion as fast as they could go.

"So, I guess that means I don't get my tech support," he said with a sigh and picked up his communicator. "I'm not entirely sure what is going on over there but I am going to assume the unicorn has returned. So, I am going to shut the shield off. Get your Aquarian star ready," Boz said into it and waited for a response, he didn't get one. For all he knew they were all killed in that one blast and he was next. Pyre horns were not known for their overwhelming sense of mercy or compassion.

"Well, with no tech support I am going to have to improvise," he said to himself and looked up at the tower. He narrowed his golden eyes and unsheathed his electric blade. "Here goes nothing," he said and thrust his blade into the computer monitor in front of him. The tower immediately began to overcharge, bright yellow sparks flew from the top of it in all directions.

"This may not have my best decision," he said to himself as the tower caught fire and the shield began to flicker out of existence above him sending streams of ocean water down in various places.

Rex was running from the fire horse when suddenly right in front of him a torrent of water fell down and he stopped before running into it. He turned around and had the unfortunate luck of having the monster be mere feet behind him. It was blinding being this close and the heat was worse.

He aimed his blaster and fired at the thing. The purple beam struck the flaming horse in the shoulder but it didn't slow its methodical march towards him.

"I should be dead by now. Any normal unicorn would have fried me. So, I know you must still be seeing this. You want me to be afraid, well I'm not going to be afraid of you or your pet, so bring it on," he yelled at the thing, and whoever was controlling it.

The horn started to burn blue once more and those dead orange eyes stared at him. Rex swallowed, but stood his ground. Rex knew that the horn was at its weakest just after it fired and timing was everything.

Suddenly another torrent of water crashed down on the both of them.

Rex was surprised and fell to his knees under the weight of the water. The flaming unicorn, on the other hand, began to scream in agony. Whatever force was controlling it seemed to break. The thing leapt back in pain as its flames burned low, revealing its charred, black skin and the red energy below it. Rex winced at seeing it and the intense steam it created burned his eyes.

The pyre horn, the vicious beast immediately realized where it was. It ran from Rex, looking for a way out of its situation, to escape the watery hell it had somehow found itself in. Rex watched as the beast ran left and right in a wild panic. With a final buzzing sound, the shield faded away and tons of water came crashing down. Rex widened his eyes and ran towards a building and dived inside.

That much water coming down at once would have shattered every bone in his body with a direct impact. The water hit the ground and instantly flooded the building. The pressure and current swept him off his feet and slammed him into the far wall. The sharp coral dug into his back but there were no serious injuries. He could only hope the others were okay.

Rex took a deep breath thanks to his charm and swam back outside. The creature of fire lay there on the ocean floor, it's ash colored skin twitching and cracks of dim red fire underneath it. It was letting out a low, agonizing cry. The commander felt sorry for the creature, in the end it was just as much a victim as all the people it killed, this time. He swam to it and landed by its head. He grabbed the charred black horn and snapped it off with surprising ease. The unicorn grunted in pain. "If you see me again, remember that I could have just left you here to suffer forever and I didn't," he said, then Rex didn't hesitate to stab the beast in the side. In seconds the beast's body crumbled into ash.

Rex picked up his communicator. "I need a head count. Is everyone still alive out there?" he asked and waited, hoping for the best but expecting some bad news.

"The robot and I are fine. Nymie and Drask are knocked out cold. Evie has a broken arm and is bleeding and we had to drag the two of them inside. We're damned lucky they weren't killed. What in the hell happened?" Tayne replied to him and Rex looked around in the dark water and it was hard to see anything around him.

"I don't have a clue, I'm just as confused as you are, let's regroup back at where the tower used to be," Rex replied and started to swim in that direction. He saw Moreno's lifeless body floating away in some weak current. The man didn't escape the crushing water, Rex couldn't help but feel bad for him. Moreno was just another of many ghosts now in the ghost town of Naber.

"I'll make whoever did this pay for it," he said and started to swim towards where the tower used to be.

Evie's blood ran down her forehead and a glowing cast was wrapped around her left arm. Tayne was carrying Nymie in his arms. Drask was floating in a glowing bubble behind Evie and the machine was walking beside her.

Boz was there at the tower, waiting for them "Well, Elrox did you no favors, or maybe he did depending on how you look at it," Boz said and managed to meet them at the ruined tower.

"Did you do this you pointy eared idiot?" Tayne screamed at him. "I saw the explosion and had no choice. I didn't know the situation so I just reacted, the way I see it is that I saved all of you from the Pyre horn," he defended his choice and narrowed his eyes at Tayne. Rex swam in from the other direction and landed on the ground.

"We could have handled it, we are in an Elroxian town, under the ocean, surrounded by water and our enemy was a god damned fire creature. It wasn't a hard problem to solve," Rex said and set foot on the soft ground. "Well I didn't hear any plans from any of you so just did what came natural," Boz said and Evie slammed her staff into the ground sending out a wave of light in all directions.

"Enough, both of you. For now, we are safe. We need to get back to the ship and put together what we know. Someone obviously wants us all dead. I suggest we find out who It is so we can find them and put them in a grave," she said in a deeper, scarier voice than she had before.

"Alright, you got your point across," Rex said and the robot looked around. "I'll stay here. Maintain the town until the authorities can clean up the mess," she said to no one. "I don't think so, you're coming with us. No one is going to come back to this town. It's a lost cause," Tayne replied to her and the robot just looked down, defeated. "We'll get you all fixed up, don't worry everything is going to be fine," Tayne replied to it, this thing obviously more advance than a typical machine.

"It looks like someone has a crush on the robot," Boz said and Tayne's red eyes shot in his direction. Boz shut up in a hurry as he took a step back.

"Voltarice, get a lock on all of us, including the robot," Rex said into his communicator. "Roger, Commander. Prepare for teleport," a voice replied. Seconds later a blue light engulfed all of them.

In seconds they were back on the ship.

"Get yourselves to sick bay, Boz," Rex said to him. The doctor didn't bother arguing or replying to that. He was sure they were fine, at least, he hoped they were. Boz couldn't believe how much damage he had done and had become resolved to fix it. Rex stepped off the platform. "Teleport them directly to Sick Bay," Rex ordered, seeing how beaten his team was. The operator did as he was told and the others disappeared. Rex decided to make his way to the bridge.

Chapter 9

Rex was sore, tired and already knew this was going to be a longer trip than he thought. He dismissed Zola with a nod. "Thank you," he said to her and she was about to say something, but decided not to and returned to her post.

He slid into his chair and he didn't do or say anything for a few seconds. Thinking about what to do next.

"Sir, where should we go now?" the helmsman asked him, Rex was snapped out of his daze, still thinking about all the things that just happened. "You know, I have no idea. As far as I know we didn't any leads down there on where to go next. You guys didn't happen to see a ship or something with a big sign on it that said bad guy is inside, did you?" Rex said and laughed about it.

"No, but when the shield disappeared we did detect a Tryon engine signature briefly before the explosion took place. It headed off towards the north. No one saw a ship," the helmsman replied to him and Rex shook his head. "And you didn't bother to tell me, why?" Rex demanded to know.

"Because Zola, well, we figured it was one of the Emerald Watch ships leaving the scene. They use the same engines," he replied and Rex glared into the viewing screen. "Track that ship, we need to find it and whoever is piloting it," he ordered and the crew began to get to work. "Yes sir, setting a due course following the Tryon particle trail, due north," he replied and started to input the commands to get underway.

The Voltarice was once again on the hunt, but Rex couldn't get the nagging feeling that they were being lead into a trap. It was always a trap when things were this easy to follow. What choice did he have?

Boz and the others appeared in the sickbay.

"Lay them on the tables carefully and I'll make sure their heads aren't cracked open," Boz said to them as he stuck his hands in the purple light sanitizer and any bacteria were wiped off in a second.

Carefully Drask and Nymie were set on the white medical tables beside one another. "For your sake I hope they'll be fine or I'm going to eat you, literally," Tayne said to the elf. "You can try, but right now get out of the way," Boz said and walked forward with a long silver device in his hand, the end of it was glowing with blue light.

Boz quickly ran it over the forehead of Nymie, "Right," he said and moved over to the other one and repeated the process. "Good news, they'll be fine in a couple of hours. No real damage was done, but unfortunately I can't do anything for their personalities," he said with a smile and walked back to the counter to put the scanner back down.

He picked up two syringes, then he noticed that Evie was facing away from them, nursing her broken arm and wounds alone. He sighed "We don't have time for that magical healing nonsense," he said to himself and walked forward.

Evie let out a small groan of pain when suddenly Boz stuck her in the right shoulder with a syringe and injected her. Evie spun around and pulled the needle out. "What the hell, damn it Boz you know I'm anti nanotech," she yelped and backed off, tossing the needle away.

"Why do you think I blindsided you, we're still on a mission and we need everyone at one hundred percent. You're going to be fine in a couple of hours without expending any extra magic, you're welcome," he replied and made his way back to the other two. With the last syringe he injected half of the nanites in each of them. "It'll take a little longer but they'll be fine in a few hours," Boz said and shrugged. "I just hope there isn't anything the scanner missed," he said to himself.

Boz looked at the robot who had followed them. "I can't do anything about you, sorry. When Drask wakes up she can repair whatever is broken and re-skin you so you look presentable," Boz said to the machine and the machine just returned a nod in silence. He almost felt sorry for the metal thing, but not quite enough. For all he knew it could have still been a bomb waiting to happen.

Tayne pulled out the tiny red chip from his pocket and looked at again. "So does anyone know where this came from or who made it?" he asked and the others looked at it. It was clear that none of them had ever seen anything like it before.

"It must be a homemade thing, I've never seen anything like it," Boz said and the vampire shook his head. "Really, you haven't seen anything like it before? I never would have guessed that," he rolled red eyes and stuck it back in his pocket. "I'm taking this down to engineering and running through the scanner," he said and it was about then they realized they were moving.

"Did anyone tell Rex something the rest of us didn't know?" Evie asked, wondering why the ship was moving and where they were going. The others were just as oblivious to the situation. "Well, at least we're all in the same boat," Evie finished when no one replied.

"I see what you did there, clever," Boz replied, but Evie just shrugged.

"Get that chip scanned as soon as you can, wherever we are going it can't be anywhere good," Boz said to Tayne.

Tayne hated people when they were so obvious and he walked out of the sick bay, rolling his eyes.

"I will deactivate until I am needed," the machine said and she walked to a corner that appeared to be rarely used and shut down. "Well that takes care of that, can we really trust the only thing we found in that ghost town, what if it's a bomb or something made for us?" Evie complained.

"Must be a pretty good bomb because nothing gets on this boat without being scanned. Any sign of a bomb physical or magical and the machine would have stayed right where it was so I think for now we can trust it," Boz replied to try and reassure her, but also trying to convince himself of the same thing. He didn't like it any more than she did.

Tayne made it to the engine room and walked to the first Elroxian he saw.

"Hey, I need your help. I need you to activate the scanner on this thing and try to find out what it is," the worker narrowed his black eyes and shook his head. "Sorry, I only take my orders from Drask, not some second-rate undead slime like you," he replied. Trask immediately grabbed the fishman by the throat and lifted him into air with his free hand with ease.

"You know, it has been something of a bad day. I think you should show a little respect for an officer of this ship, or did you not see the badge on my uniform so clearly," he said with a much more sinister voice. "I'll let the slime comment go if you decide to help me. If not, I'll kill you right here and no one will miss you," he said and waited for the walking fish to blink.

He did.

Tayne smiled and set the man down and held out the red chip. The worker took the small chip in his webbed hand and walked to a micro scanner, set the thing on the plate and turned the machine on.

Tayne crossed his arms.

"It's going to take some time, Sir, you know that the more foreign the artifact is the harder it is to scan," the man said in a very different, fearful tone. Tayne on the other hand, didn't move. "You have thirty seconds to give me something or I start tearing off fingers," he said, no longer wanting to play the nice guy for any reason at all with this one.

"Okay, okay, let me take a look," he said and looked into the viewer. "This is a homemade job but I'd recognize the chip design anywhere, it's from Mocra Industries, it's a basic bypass chip cranked up to a thousand. Placed near the central unit of any higher machine and this sucker could hack it remotely but how it works exactly, I can't tell you. I've never seen these kinds of patterns before and need more time to study it to tell you more," the worker said in a hurry.

"Mocra, so, either our bad guy works there or is really good at modification," Tayne replied. "Thanks, was that so hard? Keep working on the thing and if anything else comes up, let us know," he said to the man and walked off. The worker was afraid to do anything else other than work on this chip after that. He figured slacking off or showing disrespect would get him killed and it wasn't worth the risk.

Chapter 10

Tayne marched down the halls and moved straight to the bridge with surprising speed. It didn't take him long to get there and less than a second to get to the Commander's chair.

"Rex, I have a lead on where to go next," he said and Rex looked back at him, to anyone else it looked as if Tayne just teleported out of thin air. Rex knew better. "How are the others doing?" he asked, ignoring the chance at a lead.

"Boz says they'll be fine, but I found a chip and had it scanned. It came from Mocra Industries. It's a custom bypass chip. I think we should go to Mr. Mocra's glittering factory and ask him a few questions," Tayne said and Rex looked out the viewing screen into the darkness. "Yeah, because anyone could have modified a chip in their own garage, I don't think it's a good lead," Rex replied.

"Normally, I'd agree with you, but where else should we look?" Tayne asked. Rex smiled in response.

"We caught someone fleeing the scene so we are chasing them down, you might have noticed we are moving. They are no match for our ship so we should be on them in a few minutes. We can see what's going on once we catch this guy," Rex said and Tayne didn't like this idea at all.

"It's a trap, you know that right. People wouldn't just escape like that," he said and Rex shook his head.

"Maybe they just screwed up and got caught like most stupid criminals do," he countered him. Knowing Tayne was likely right but changing course on a choice would only demonstrate weakness to the rest of the crew and he couldn't have that right now.

Tayne shook his head in disagreement but knew it was nearly impossible to change Rex's mind once it was made up. "Besides, Tayne, when have we ever run away from a good trap?" Rex asked with a smile. Tayne just narrowed his eyes. "Never, I guess," he replied.

"Sir, coming up on the speeder now," the helmsman said to him and put it on screen. It was, in comparison, a tiny green ship made for one person, but not belonging to any of the Emerald Watch, that much was obvious just by looking at it.

"Activate the winch and drag this guy into our holding dock, I'll meet him there, Tayne, you're with me," Rex said and stood up. The both of them walked off the bridge.

The Voltarice fired a red beam from its side. The small speeder was taken and frozen in place immediately. In seconds it was being dragged backwards and a few minutes later the ship was placed inside the holding dock. Rex and Tayne watched it rise up from the airlock into the holding dock, the sea water. "It's a good thing the winch kills their engines," Rex said. "Yeah, I guess," Tayne replied and wasn't quite sure why he said half the things he did at random sometimes.

"So, should you knock, or should I?" Rex asked and pulled his blaster out just to be ready for anything. Admittedly he knew he should have done this before the ship was even inside, that would have been the smart thing to do.

"This is your deal, you knock. I'll watch and hope the thing doesn't blow up, I might laugh though," he said and Rex shook his head. "Fine, I'll go first but you get the next one," he said and walked forward towards the hatch on the side and knocked on it quickly.

"Hello, I am the Commander of the Voltarice. I am sorry to inconvenience you but you were seen trying to get away from a crime scene and we need to ask you some questions, we tried to hail you but you didn't respond," Rex said and lied about that last part, he didn't try to hail the ship at all nor did he care about that. There was no response.

"Did anyone even scan this ship for life or anything, do I need to do everything around here, by Taro's beard this is annoying," he said and knocked on the hatch again when this time the seal hissed and broke open. Rex jumped back as the door did this.

"Jumpy much, Rex?" Tayne asked with a wicked smile but unhooked is shotgun just in case.

The ship fully opened and a man stepped out wearing a black robe, carrying a staff made out two long leg bones made from trolls. "It's a damn necromancer," Rex said and pointed his blaster at the man who in turned created a sphere of black energy in his free hand.

"What are you doing way out here, don't you freaks usually hang out in the Northern Kingdom?" Tayne demanded, he had a particular hate for these people. The man removed his black hood and revealed his self-inflicted facial scars.

"It's a new age human. It's a new age for all of us. The unicorns are rising again and we can't ignore the signs," he said in a raspy voice that barely sounded like anything alive should. "The signs that you created, yeah, can't ignore them. All I want to know is how you managed to control a unicorn," Rex said and the necromancer smiled, the skin on his face cracked open and bled as he did this.

"I did not control anything. I am only a deliverer of the new God's will. Hail the Black Unicorn," the man screamed and began to make his move to attack. "No," Tayne said and fired his shotgun first. The deep red and purple blast struck the necromancer and knocked him to the ground in one shot. "He's not dead, Rex, do you really want to keep this monster on board as a prisoner or not, decide right now," Tayne said and Rex pointed his blaster at the necromancer's head and fired.

"Hell no, I don't," he replied and kicked the morbid staff away from the body and watched it fade into dust as he did. The necromancer's body also crumbled into dust as if it had been dead for a thousand years and the dust faded away into nothing. "They usually don't do that," Tayne said, "No, it was a dead skin messenger, another damned puppet," Rex replied in disgust.

Tayne was the first one to step inside the machine, but he did so very carefully.

Inside was filled with pages made out of skin from various races and all colors, plastered everywhere. Each one had the image of a unicorn on it, different variations of each kind and what he could only assume to be spells written on each page in language he couldn't understand or even make sense out of any of it.

"It's a room full of crazy in here Rex, I don't recommend you come in, or you know, anyone else," he said. Then Tayne saw something he did recognize. The symbol of the Delrax Cult engraved on the one bare piece of green metal on the wall. It looked a lot like a black sun, but instead of light rays, tendrils coming off a core. Simple, yet unforgettable. Even if one had never seen it before, they would know that it meant something bad.

He'd seen it many times before with Necromancers that came through the Morglands looking for supplies.

"This ship at least belongs to the Delrax Cult," Tayne said as he made his way out before he discovered anything else horrible about this ship. "So, the forbidden god has something to do with unicorns? I mean I wouldn't be surprised if old squid face did, but there is no proof Delrax even exists besides a delusional group of necromancers like this one," Rex said and Tayne nodded.

"Well, these people, if you can call them that, think it does and that's enough for me. After the Blade incident and the Gods actually showing up, who knows what else is lurking out there? I just don't know what he was doing all the way out here. Necromancers don't like the water," Tayne added and took another look into the ship as Rex did too and unlike the vampire, Rex nearly gagged at what he saw.

"How many people were killed for this, whatever I am looking at?" Rex wondered out loud and Tayne didn't even want to guess. The skin pages were basically wall paper. "We need to let Evie take a look at this, maybe she can see something we didn't," Rex said and backed away from the vile ship in a hurry.

"Oh yeah, she's going to love that job for sure," Tayne added and there was only a minute of silence between them as they stared at it. Finally, Rex picked up his communicator.

"Evie, I'm going to need you to come up holding bay two, I have a job for you," he said into it. "On my way," she replied almost immediately. Within seconds she was there in a dim column of blue light.

Immediately she saw the black, empty robe of the necromancer on the ground. "What in the hell happened down here?" she asked, her arm was already healed from Boz's Nano shot. "We think a Delrax cultist was on the ship, but it's what we found inside, you're not going to like it," Rex said to her and took another deep breath. Evie turned and looked at the small ship and walked towards it.

She could smell the death coming out of the hatch long before she got there and blamed the nanites for messing with her senses. Something like this should have alerted her magically right away, yet she felt nothing and still did this close to it.

"Oh Elrox, what in the hell did this freak do?" she asked as she looked in to see all the skin pages pinned to the walls. "We just need to know what it says, if you can't figure it out we are sending this thing to crime labs and they can take it from there," Rex said to her and Evie hated what she was looking at.

"Alright, I understand. I'll do my best to figure it out but no promises," she said, took a deep breath and walked inside. "I sure hope she figures something out," Tayne said quietly to mostly himself.

Evie stepped inside of the Necromancer's ship that was full to the brim with insanity. The first reaction she had was the same one she had when it came all necromancers, disgust. "Vile," she said to herself, but reminded herself what she was here to do. She waved her hand and summoned a purple light.

"Gyo" she said and hoped for the best. The purple light spread through the chamber and waited. Slowly, the arcane codes engraved on the flaps of skin began to form something that resembled a language. Evie tilted her head and tried to read the words, but she only knew what the language was and not how to read it. "It's Jurlian," she said to herself in a huff.

"Always Jurlian with these people," she complained and got back out of the chamber.

"It's typical Necromancer Code, Jurlian," she said to the two of them. Tayne shook his head "I hate that the Necromancers use a primitive, dead language and can't they make things easy for us?" he asked no one and Rex nodded in agreement. "Well, we don't have any experts on the dead language on board. We need to port this and everything on it to labs back in the city," Rex said and looked at Tayne.

"We're going to Mocra Industries," Rex finished and walked away. Evie shuddered, she hated all the things about Mocra, but most mages tended to because of the science and mystical battle that was ever present.

"Fine, but don't expect me to be very nice about it," she said quietly as he left. "Context I suppose, I found a chip on the bot that is directly connected to the company. We're going there but we don't need to be nice. We have questions that need answers," Tayne said and Evie smiled, she was happy for that, at least.

Chapter 11

In the sick bay, Nymie and Drask were already awake. "I still don't know what happened, I all remember was a wall of water then everything went black," Drask said, rubbing her forehead. "Same here. Everything was bad then it went to terrible, the sky fell in and I remember panic," Nymie agreed and Boz walked over to him. "Well it's good to see you're alright. Some idiot panicked when they saw the explosions of the Pyre horn and deactivated the shield without warning anyone," Boz said to them and Drask narrowed her eyes.

"If I find out who did that I am going to kill them," she said angrily. "No worries, the tower fell on the man who did it and killed him instantly," Boz added and turned away. "Well, good, that saves me the trouble of doing it myself," Nymie agreed with Drask about killing him and Boz took a deep breath.

"In lighter news we picked up a stowaway, a damaged utility robot that needs repairing," Boz said and

Drask sat up. "Really, that'll give me something to do, why are we moving?" she asked and Boz shrugged his shoulders. "I don't know. You'll have to ask Rex or someone because I've been stuck in here putting you two back together," he replied to her and kept his cool as best as he could.

Nymie stood up and stretched to make sure everything still worked. Boz pretended not to notice her. "You two better go get caught up and do whatever it is we're doing next," he said and Drask too stood up. "Yeah, I'll go see about this robot we brought on board. It'll give me something to do," she said and walked out. Boz turned to face Nymie.

"Hey, if you're not busy later we could get something to eat. I mean barring any horrible emergencies or anything," he asked her and tried not to show that he was nervous. She looked down as she approached him. "Sure, why not, I'll contact you when I know I'm free," she replied to him with a slight smile.

Despite being tall for an elf, Nymie made him look short. She was almost eight feet tall and he liked that. She walked off and he did his best not to watch her leave. The sliding doors closed behind her and Boz sighed, he only hoped now no one decided to mention the shield tower incident and ruin this for him. He was kicking himself for lying about all of this but he really didn't want to die at the hands of someone he liked.

Boz had other plans, at least, in his own mind he saw things far in the future that for now only existed in dreams.

Drask made her way to engineering and found a worker sitting on a bench rubbing his throat by the door, he looked scared. She knew who it was right way. "Niver, why are you just sitting there doing nothing," she asked him without looking. "That vampire Tayne encouraged me to scan some chip he found aggressively, with his hand. He nearly strangled me," he said, but couldn't bring himself to look at her.

"It won't happen again, take the rest of the day off, unless I need you," Drask said and walked away from him. "The chip is in scanner three, it's about half way done," Niver replied as he walked out of the room. "Oh, someone teleported that machine in here, it gives me the creeps," Niver said as he walked away.

Drask walked to scanner three and looked inside. "Well a Mocra control chip. Looks like a mod job," she said to herself but didn't exactly know how it worked. Hello, I am Unie, how are you?" the machine asked and Drask jumped, she didn't even hear it approach.

"So you are. Um, welcome aboard the Voltarice and man what happened to you?" she asked looking at the damaged, burned form machine.

"I was attacked by a unicorn. I was damaged," Unie replied. Drask figured that, she was hoping for more information. "Okay, well I have a repair pod you can use over here you should come with me so we can make you whole again," Drask said and began to walk. The machine followed her. The two of them came to a silver pod and with a push of a button it slid open.

"Please, enter. Don't be afraid. I won't dismantle you. I happen to like machines," she said almost nervously. The machine stepped in. "I know what fear is, but I don't think I know how to express it. I will trust you," she said, turned around. The silver door closed. Drask pushed a few more buttons and the process began. "Good as new in no time," she said.

Nymie walked on to the bridge and stood beside Rex's chair. "Hey, what are we planning now?" she asked Rex couldn't help but notice her show up and wasn't surprised. "Glad to see you're alright. We are on our way to Mocra Industries to ask the ones in charge a few questions. Tayne found a chip connected to them. Someone modified it and we need to know who," Rex said and Nymie shook her head.

"Wouldn't a phone call work just fine for this, it feels like a wasted trip to me," she replied and Rex laughed.

"No, we were almost killed by someone who figured out how to control a unicorn, we have to do this in person. I'll let you ask the questions if you want. Also, we captured a Delrax necromancer, but once I shot him in the head he kind of lost his ability to answer questions. Inside the ship was filled with Jurlian text that we had to send to a crime lab to figure out what it said, you don't want to know what it was printed on," Rex said to her and Nymie shuddered.

"Delrax tend to be the worst, but not all necromancers are bad. I've known a couple of good ones here and there," she replied with a smile.

Rex just smirked, "I'll bet you did," he replied and continued. "It's going to take about three hours before we get there. We have it covered up here, go take a break or something if I need you I'll be sure to call everyone," Rex said and Nymie nodded. "Sounds good to me," she said, turned around and walked off the bridge. She lifted her communicator.

"Hey Boz, I'm free right now. If you're still up for it I'll meet you in the mess hall in a few minutes. I'm on my way there now," she said to him.

"I'll be there very soon," he replied to her.

Chapter 12

Boz and Nymie met in the mess hall at about the same time. Boz waved slightly and the two of them met at a table near the center of the room and sat down. "So, how are you?" Boz asked her and Nymie shook her head. "Really, we just talked like ten minutes ago and this is your opening line, what's the matter?" she stared down at him and Boz blinked.

"Uh, no I'm actually just, well I ran out of things to say. I'm not that great at talking you know, it's a flaw of mine," Boz said as the holographic menu appeared in front of them and the two of them began pressing what they wanted.

Boz only wanted something light, her, on the other hand began to push several buttons. "Damn, you sure eat a lot," Boz said out loud without thinking. "Yeah, you don't talk much, I eat too much. You of all people should know that Troll biology requires a lot of calories to keep going, at least ten thousand a day according to science," she smiled and Boz felt like he got a lucky break, he didn't mind a woman who could eat a lot.

Boz was about to say something when all of the sudden the whole ship was rocked to the left. Nymie reached across the table and grabbed Boz before he could fly to the opposite wall. "What in the hell just hit us?" Boz asked, his arm was in pain due to her grip but hitting the wall would have been a lot worse. Six others were not so lucky as they slammed against the medal wall.

"All senior officers to the bridge, we have a problem," Rex said over the radio. "A problem, really, I never would have guessed. Looks like lunch is going to have to wait," Nymie said and with ease stood up as the ship began to right itself. "Come on let's there before there is another attack," Boz said the obvious, Nymie ignored him as they made their way to the door.

"Six injured in the mess hall, get some teams up here. I need to go to the bridge and I will join when I can," Boz said into his communicator before leaving.

Drask was looking at the chip when suddenly all the alarms began to blare and everything tilted to the left. "What the hell," she said and hung on to a rail. She looked around and saw that everyone else did too. The ship was already righting itself when she moved towards the status console. "Magical energy detected? What in the hell hit us?" she asked herself as she read to herself.

"Drask, I'm not sure how they did it but we have four necro cruisers surrounding us, our wards are holding for now but we're going to need weapons online," Rex said to her through a speaker. "Weapons aren't online, who in the hell is running this boat, who doesn't have their weapons online in the out waters all the time?" Drask complained but didn't waste any time. "Get the missiles and laser banks online, now," she ordered and her crew scrambled to get to work.

Tayne and Evie were walking towards the bridge when the attack occurred. Evie slammed into Tayne but he was able to support and hold her up. "Get us to the bridge," Tayne said to her and Evie tapped her staff on the floor. Instantly they were out of the hall and on the bridge, the blue light faded away. "We have four necro cruisers. When I broke their toy, they must have got some kind of a signal, we can take them but these are some pissed off wizards," Rex said and Evie walked towards the viewing screen.

"Can we talk to them?" she asked and Rex honestly didn't even think about that. "Sure, we can try, hail them," Rex ordered and Tayne ran to the communications station. "Open up all the channels just to make sure we get through to them," Tayne ordered. "Yes Sir," the officer replied and did so. "Talk when ready," the man said.

"This is the Voltarice hailing the four necro cruisers that are currently shooting at us, we might have some kind of misunderstanding. Could you please talk to us so we don't have to wipe you out, your ships are no match for mine and you know it," Rex said.

For a minute, there was no response.

"This is Delrax's sacred water, leave now or be destroyed," a raspy voice replied to them. Rex, nor anyone else really knew too much about the cult so they had no idea what they held sacred. "Sorry, we didn't know, actually nobody held these waters. I have a question, before we go what do you know about controlling unicorns?" Rex asked them and again, silence for a full minute.

"Nothing, now leave or be destroyed. We may not be a match for your ship but you cannot stand against the whole fleet," the voice responded and Rex rolled his eyes. "I get it, but we had a run in with one of your group and they fled the scene of a particularly vicious unicorn attack and there was a primitive glass golem there too, so if you didn't do it, someone is framing you. Thought you might like to know," Rex replied to them. He wasn't going to mention the chip.

"We will send an envoy to your ship once you leave to discuss this more with you, follow the ship out and we will talk," the voice replied "Lead the way," Rex replied and nodded to Tayne to shut off the communications. "You're clear," Tayne replied a second later.

"Well look at that, a reasonable Necromancer," Rex said and Evie turned. "They aren't all bad, they just follow a different path is all. You have to understand that most of them want to be left alone. There are a few extremists out there who make them all look bad, let's follow them out of where ever we are and keep the peace," she said and Rex didn't buy much of it, but didn't argue with her.

"Alright, follow that ship and let's see where we end up," Rex said and didn't know what was coming next, but he was prepared for anything. He'd was going to be upset if the envoy ended up to be a pack of ghouls.

The Voltarice followed the much smaller necro cruiser for twenty-five minutes. Rex didn't know what was going on besides just following this thing and keeping an eye out for anymore traps. "We are here, disable your wards and I will come over to talk to you," the raspy voice came over the radio. The ones who were on the bridge looked at one another.

"Evie, if you'd do the honors," Rex said to her and she sighed. "Please don't make me regret this," she said to herself and closed her eyes to deactivate the outer wards. Seconds later a column of black smoke appeared and when it faded away a man was standing there in an actual nice, black suit. "Nice ship you have here," he said to all of them in a very different voice than what was on the communicator. "Thanks, but let's make this quick. What do you know?" Rex was quick to get to the point.

"Right, A few months ago a sect of our organization reportedly discovered a blade when the others were unsealed. But this one remained sealed. It was in a cave deep in the black waters. On the way back home, they were attacked by a Hydro Horn, as you'd call it. This sect was mostly wiped out but one remained and out of desperation, presented the blade. The unicorn immediately stopped its attack," the man in the suit said to him and the others were suspicious. "How do you know so much?" Rex asked.

"My home town was attacked and destroyed by a herd of Hydro horns six days ago lead by some maniac who seemed to control them. He had the blade with him, but it was still sealed. I, and some others escaped, but I saw the whole thing and everyone heard the maniac tell the story to us before he attacked," the man said and looked down.

"Sixty people were slaughtered and their bodies were dragged away, I don't know why, but I know unicorns usually eat their victims, not take them away," he added and rubbed his left arm. "So a necromancer is behind all of this, did you get a name?" Tayne asked and the man looked at him.

"The chill weed actually claimed to actually be Delrax. I am sure our God wouldn't kill us, at least I don't think so," he replied.

"Alright, thank you for your time, we'll investigate this and if you're attacked again call us and we will be there," Rex said and tossed a communicator to him.

"It's always on, someone will always be on the other end," he finished and the Necromancer caught it. "A surface dweller would be willing to help us? You're weird, I'll inform the others of your generosity," he said and Rex nodded. The very human looking necromancer disappeared in another column of smoke. Just as Boz and Nymie walked through the door to the bridge.

"Mocra Corp and an unknown Blade. What's the connection?" Tayne asked and none of them knew or wanted to know. "I suggest we find out, but it looks like the deeper water is their realm. I suggest we just take the surface route and play it safe," Evie suggested and Rex was thinking the same thing.

"Take us up," he ordered and soon the Voltarice was rising from the depths of the Yalo ocean once more into the sunlight.

"Mocra is only about seventeen miles off the coast, we can be there in about twenty minutes if we take our time," Nymie said as she took over the helm, still hungry and irritable but figured she should do something now that she was here.

"Well then what are we waiting for, let's go," Rex ordered and Nymie pushed the ship into action.

"Drask, keep those weapons powered up and check for any damage," Rex said after another communicator appeared in his hand. "Will do, Sir, just keep a better watch out for trouble in the future," she said and was obviously annoyed. "You got it, I'll do my best to not get us shot again," he replied and put the radio away.

"Evie, put the wards back up if you would please," Rex asked more than ordered her. "Already on it, Sir, what if Delrax really is walking among us? If there is another blade out there and it's unsealed, couldn't it mean the end of the world would start all over again? And why wasn't this blade unsealed with the rest?" Evie asked and Rex didn't know much about it, the news out of the North suggested the threat was over.

"If there is an evil god out there we'll just have to hope ours are stronger and stand with us if we need them when the time comes," Rex said the only thing he could think of.

"I hope they stand with us if it's true," Boz said, despite not being a fan of the gods or magic very much but their existence now was undeniable, however they still felt weak to him because even if the event had come to an end, nothing had changed.

Rex didn't know very much than when he started this whole thing but he was hoping a stop at Mocra Tower was going to fix all of that. He had a feeling there was more than just magic involved with this.

Chapter 13

There on the shoreline of the Yalo ocean it stood, like a glittering green emerald monument to progress and all things science, but the whole thing stood alone. "I see it on the radar, should I blow it up now or later," Drask called in over the communicator. Rex smiled as he looked at the golden letters that spelled Mocra down the side so no one would could mistake who owned it.

"No, not yet. I am sure they know we are here by now and besides. No evidence. I'll need you to come with me, bring the chip. Evie, Nymie come with me.

The rest of you stay on board and make sure to keep a close eye on anything that seems out of place," Rex said to them and Tayne smiled. "You know you can count on me to keep an eye out, that's me, typical watchdog," he replied with great sarcasm, imagining all the things he could be doing right now, like sleeping.

"Well then have someone else do it, but if something does happen even you are going to feel bad about it," Rex replied and Tayne rolled his eyes. "Yeah, yeah, don't worry about it. I'll keep watch," Tayne replied.

"Mocra is a horrible business. I don't understand why so many people buy into it," Evie said. "Well they helped build this ship and a lot of the tech on this world, them and a few others. The royal families invested in them and now we have what we do," Nymie replied, she was excited to come here because Mocra made some of the things she enjoyed the most and didn't want to believe they were connected to this in any way.

She also wasn't about to tell Evie that, however. The three of them walked to the elevator and got inside. Rex pressed a red button.

The elevator stopped and they got out, met by Drask who had the chip in a small plastic bag to keep it safe. "Let's go say hello," the dwarf said to them and they walked to the transporter platform. "You're coming too?" Evie asked. "Yeah, I am. Mocra has some pretty high port shielding, however I talked the CEO into taking the fast track to the head office at the top," she said and Rex smiled.

"Good deal," Rex replied.

"Get us down there," Rex said to the operator and in seconds they found themselves standing in the tower's shadow, from here it looked much more sinister from the air and something about the Voltarice being in the sky near it didn't make them feel much better. "I thought you said fast track?" Rex asked. Drask just shrugged. "As fast as I could get it," she replied.

"Hello, hello!" a voice cried out. A man in a bright green suit came out to meet them.

"I'm Rence Mocra, CEO of, well this. So, what can I do for such esteemed Unicorn Hunters on this fine day," he asked and had a sinister smile for an elf, the twinkle of his red eyes didn't make any of them feel better. Rex didn't trust him.

"We're going to get straight to the point, we found this on a bot and it belongs to you, or it was at least modified by someone who has connections to this place. Controller chips aren't something normal people can get their hands on," Rex said and Drask stepped forward, holding the chip out for Rence to take. The elf tilted his head and took the bag.

"Oh yeah, this came from here alright. The structure of the chip almost looks organic," he said at first glance. "This isn't the first one we have seen," Rence replied and frowned, continuing. "I thought we could keep this under wraps. You should come with me I want to show you all something you might find interesting," he said, turned around and began to walk inside the tower.

"No guards, wouldn't a big wig like this have personal protection?" Evie whispered to Rex. "I wouldn't be surprised if we are being watched right now, let's go see what he has to show us and be ready for anything," Rex whispered back and the group quickly caught up with the elf.

Rence and the others didn't even bother to stop at security check points. All of the guards just let them through, even saluting them as they passed by. Rex returned the salute, he knew that Unicorn hunters were respected and to see this many high-ranking ones in one spot was rare. The others didn't bother, but Rex's acknowledgment was more than enough for them.

Rence stopped before the elevator, turned around and looked Nymie up and down. "We'll take the service elevator, I forget just how big you trolls can get, not that I mind, I just didn't expect. Well you understand right?" he asked her and she looked down.

"Yeah, I get that a lot. Lead the way," she said and Rence smiled and opened the elevator, the thing was obviously made for transporting very large items.

The doors opened and they got in. "So, what are we in for?" Rex asked him and Rence just smiled. "Something you'll appreciate, I wanted to wait to reveal this but, I figure in order to explain the chip, the whole story needs to be revealed," he replied in his same upbeat tone.

The elevator ride was a long one, they kept going down and it felt like there wasn't going to be an end but suddenly the doors opened to a large, well-lit chamber. They walked forward to see large tanks lining the walls of the room.

Inside each tank was a unicorn in stasis.

"What in the hell is this?" Evie said out loud, shocked at the sight.

"It's unlimited energy. Unicorns are extradimensional beasts that never lose their connection to their home. I found a way to catch and harness their power for the good of everyone," he said and turned around with a smile.

"You're insane, what if they break out so close to populated areas, you risk killing thousands," Rex immediately said and reached for his blaster on instinct. "This program has been going on in secret for three years. The hardest part is catching the monsters but I pay some hunters, who will remain nameless, to help with the task," he said, that smile never left.

"You don't understand, Unicorns gather power the longer they stay in this dimension. Taking one out fast is important. The longer it stays here the worse it gets. They've been here for three years or more," Drask said and shuddered at the thought.

"Yes, I understand perfectly, their power increases and so does their energy output. Without this we would face an energy crisis, there would be a social breakdown. You can trust me. However not all the employees agreed with this plan," Rence said and that smile finally left his face.

"About the time the blade incident took place Albert Grayson, one of the chief scientists of the project, apparently lost his mind. He kept saying the unicorns were screaming into his brain and eventually we found him, dead in his office. He cut his wrists and made a terrible mess," Rence said with a sigh and continued, "then three days later his body disappeared. That was a few weeks ago and ever since we've been finding spy bots with similar chips on them like the one you found. We don't know what to make of it either and were about to come to you for some help. Do you know if unicorns are telepathic at all?" he asked them and finally finished.

"Some of them are, but then again I've only tried to banish them back to their world and not really deal with what they were thinking," Nymie replied and the others agreed with that. "Psycho Horns, Mimic Horns are telepathic for sure," Evie replied.

"Well the blade incident changed everything. The unicorns here are increasing in power seven times faster than they should be, the containment is fine but we don't know what is going on. That friends, is all we know," Rence said to them, Rex couldn't tell If he was telling the truth or not but he sure looked like he was.

Evie couldn't help but feel sorry for the beasts, despite them being straight up killers no matter what form they took, nothing deserved to be locked up like this. "I don't care if there is an energy crisis looming, we need to banish these things as soon as we can. To walk away would be a serious violation of our code and jobs," Evie said, tightening her grip on the staff.

"I'm sorry but these things are Mocra property and damaging them would be a direct attack on our company, we, I, cannot allow that," the elf said, looking at her, knowing exactly how the Elroxian felt seemed to make him smile.

"You know, today it might be fine, but someday you won't be able to contain them and it will take a lot to stop them when they get out. I don't know how much help we are going to be," Drask said to him, raising a valid point. "Maybe, but if that happens I'll be fine. I'm hardly ever down here so I am not the one that'll need to be saved," he said with a smile and started to walk back towards the elevator.

"Well, at least you'll be okay, I guess it's all fine then," Nymeria replied, disgusted with his lack of concern for life. Rence almost looked back, but stopped himself.

"Albert Grayson's body has disappeared. I've already planned for all of his stuff to be teleported to your ship, he really didn't have anyone to give it too and, well, we didn't want to tell the Emerald Watch or the cops. So, we kept it in storage. Investigate and see if you can find anything we didn't. We didn't find anything of importance but we aren't exactly super elite hunters like yourselves, maybe you'll catch something we missed," Rence said to them, changing the subject.

"I'm sure we will," Rex replied and there was a short span of silence between them. "Well I have work to do as do you so this is where we will part ways. Use the elevator and please leave the same way you came int," the elf said, pushed a button on his wrist as the hologram disappeared.

"Holy snorb, it was a hologram, I couldn't even tell," Nymie said and Drask just nodded, but she couldn't tell either honestly. "Let's just get out of here before we decide to do something we'll regret," Evie said, tapped her staff on the ground and in seconds they were all back on the bridge.

Chapter 14

"Well that was fast, learn anything?" Tayne asked them.

"Yeah, more than I wanted to," Rex replied and sat down in his chair. "He's keeping unicorns down there, they are powering most, if not all of the settlements behind the wall," Nymie said and Boz's eyes widened. "What, no that's not good," he said and it appeared that he had said the obvious "Yeah, I think we all thing that," Drask replied.

"I mean, no, unicorn energy is naturally corruptive. I've been studying it for a few years now and their natural energy is alien to our dimension. It warps everything they are around, it's a naturally occurring chaos field in effect," he clarified what he meant. "So that's the reason everything goes to hell when one hangs around one area too long, and here I thought it was just because they smelled that bad," Drask replied.

"He's kept at least ten of them that we could see in his basement for three years and they increased their energy output recently," Drask replied and Boz started to go into a panic attack.

"Whoa, calm down man, you're not helping anyone by freaking out right now," Evie said to him but Boz glared at her. "Everyone is in danger, anyone who uses a light, anyone who uses anything powered by the energy is in serious trouble or they will be. We have to at least warn them that they are being poisoned," he said in response.

"Okay, I'll contact Lexam, you guys need to get to Grayson's stuff and check it over for anything we can find. I think he's somehow behind all of this mess but we need to see what we can find out," and continued. "Grayson's stuff is in holding deck two. If you don't find anything, I don't know what we are going to do next so good luck," Rex said to them and they nodded and made their way out of the bridge.

Rex sat in his chair and pushed a few buttons that were on the side of it. For a few seconds there was no answer. Then the King's advisor, a squirrelly Elroxian by the name of Orma answered the call, she looked at him through the viewing screen.

"Commander Rex, what can I do for you?" she asked him, nervously.

Rex took a breath before he chose his words.

"I need you to get the King on the line as soon as possible, this is an emergency," he replied to her. "I'm sorry but the King is in a meeting right now. I can relay a message if you want," she said and Rex shook his head. "A message okay, tell him that Mocra industries is using Unicorn energy to power most of the Kingdom and that energy is dangerous, everyone needs to stop using their lights. Anything connected to electric power because it's not electricity," he said to her and continued.

"The energy output has been climbing and if what I think is going to happen, does, we, everyone is going to be in for a world of pain," Rex said to her and Orma's eyes widened.

"Oh Elrox, I didn't know. I'll go tell the king right now, be safe out there. Is there any time line to this disaster?" she asked him.

"No, we don't know when the surge is going to come but it is going to come so you need to hurry. Our best guess, less than twenty-four hours," Rex made something up, unicorn energy was almost impossible to detect without magic assistance or visual aids of the area around it.

"Okay, I'll tell him right now," she said and shut off her communications. Rex sighed and hoped he wasn't too late.

Tayne and Drask were in cargo bay two and both of them were going through everything Mocra had sent up to them. "While I have you here, did you try to strangle one of my department members?" Drask asked him straight out.

"The guy was getting in my way and I didn't have any patience, so yes I did but he didn't die so I figure it all turned out alright," he replied to her and she glared at him. "If you ever do it again I'll tear your dead heart out myself and eat it, threatening my people is not okay, ever. I need all of them to make sure the ship, the thing you and I are on, keeps flying, understand," Drask said as she started pulling random documents out of a dusty box. Tayne smiled, but she didn't see that.

"You got it boss, next time I'll just throw them off the ship so they can't cry about it," he replied and opened a box. Drask knew he got the message and dropped it. "This Grayson guy was pretty smart, I can't make heads or tails out of any of this stuff," Tayne said as he read some of the papers.

"What's a Unocite?" he asked her and Drask shook her head. "It's basically a measurement of energy, very small," she replied to him the short version. "Al here was obsessed with them, he must have been down there with those things constantly. Each paper is measured by the hour, every hour," Tayne said and pulled out a whole stack of papers that were filled with numbers all identical besides the number of Unocites going up each page.

"They said he was the chief scientist, I'd expect him to keep very good notes. Looks like you got the boring pile," Drask said as she pulled out blood stained papers and tried to read them.

"Unicorn voices tell me that the path is open and the time is now. Give up my life to open the door to the path and free yourself from the world of the Gods," Drask read out loud and didn't know what it meant.

"This is not the first person I've heard of that sacrificed themselves to a unicorn for whatever reason, but none of them ever left a note like this," Tayne replied to it and shrugged. "What path, what door. I've never heard of anything like it. He wrote down things about voices but they all seem to be saying the same thing, is it possible his mind was corrupted by over exposure to the energy?" Drask asked.

"A telepathic unicorn isn't new, but usually they just use their power to lure victims. I've never even heard of such a thing like this before," he replied and shook his head. "Is it possible the black unicorn is talking across the barrier, are we being played somehow?" Drask thought to herself out loud.

"It is possible, if such a thing exists," Tayne replied but she didn't hear him, lost in her own thoughts.

"I'm going to run some of these numbers through the computers back in Engineering, you two have fun," Drask said and left to go to her station.

"Yeah, fun," Tayne replied as she left.

Orma burst into the meeting room, out of breath and afraid.

"Rex just reported in. He says Mocra Corp is using Unicorn power to supply energy to most of the kingdom, if not all of it and a disaster is coming in twenty four hours. Rex says to warn everyone to get off the grid, cut your power, he says you need to warn the people. Get everyone to disconnect," she said in the middle of the meeting. The King smiled at the district heads he was meeting with at the time. "Excuse me," he said and turned around and stared at her.

"First off, knock first, second of all thanks for the warning. I'm going to warn the public however, I am going to shut off all non-essential power grids just to be sure. I will not allow unicorn energy in my kingdom," Lexam said to her and dismissed her with a nod. Orma quickly closed the doors and left the people in the room.

"I don't know what is going on but I do trust Commander Rex, if he says it's true I am believing him. You're needed in your districts. Tell them to remain calm," Lexam ordered and one by one they teleported out of the room. The king stood up and looked out the glass window from where he could see most of the surface side of the kingdom from here through the mist. Millions of glittering lights just under the eternal layer of fog.

"I have to prevent this," he said to himself and walked out of the room into his throne room that wasn't far away. He picked up his phone he left on the arm of the coral throne and pushed a few buttons. "Hi, yeah. Listen. I need you to cut off all power to the kingdom. I was just informed that Unicorn energy was coming through the wires from Mocra, and not electricity. Yeah, we need to stop this as soon as we can," Lexam said and continued. "Thanks, get it done as soon as you can, I know it's going to be tough be we need to keep power to emergency services by all means possible, do your best," he said and hung up the phone.

"Damn you Mocra, how did you end up using such vile sources of energy, you should have just come to me first we could have avoided what comes next," Lexam said as the lights around him went dark, but only for a few seconds as the generators switched on. Lexam made another phone call.

"I'm going to need a telepath up here in the throne room, I have a message to relay to the population and get Rence to the castle as soon as you can, we need to talk," he said into it and hung up. "Elrox help us all, I hope it wasn't too late," he said to himself and couldn't believe just how much he had trusted Rence and so blindly, too. It was not a time to get mad at himself, now was the time for action.

Rex watched as from the bridge of the ship as he saw most of the lights in the distance shut off in massive sections at a time one after another. "Good, he got the message and actually listened," he said to himself when suddenly a voice came into his, and everyone's mind.

"This is an emergency telepathic message. The blackout you are experiencing is for your own safety. I was just informed that the energy you are all using is drawn from Unicorns, I will urge you not to panic. We believe we caught it before any damage could be done, please stand by for more details," Lexam's voice faded from his mind. "Not much for explaining things, is he?" Rex commented to no one and hoped his people would discover something out before things got worse.

He took his phone out of his side pocket, but there was no service anymore. Now he could only hope for the best and put it back.

Nymie was reading the digital files on Albert's computer but it didn't have anything obviously useful. Albert Grayson didn't seem to have any connections to anyone. All of his stuff was here but the body was missing. She was sure Mocra had something to do with it, she didn't trust him at all.

He was surely hiding something from them despite showing them the unicorns being used as a source of power. Nymie was flipping through endless files, all numbered and mostly meaningless. Then one that didn't fit came on the list. She clicked on a file that read 'birthday party' last opened four weeks ago.

She didn't get the feeling that Rence's team investigated this file so she opened it and it only had one message on it.

"The body is ready. The spirit is ready. The portal will be opened so the two can become one. I give my life for the true master of the world and everything on it. You will not be disappointed. We await the promised surge in our place of safety, we wait for the foretold sign and the end to begin," she read out loud and didn't quite understand it.

"Sounds like someone's been drinking too much of the crazy aid," Tayne replied as he heard it, but didn't take his eyes off of the papers he was looking at,"

Then Lexam's message came into her head the same time it did for the rest of them. She tried to block it out as she read the message again. Then it clicked.

"Wait, if they cut of all the power, where does the energy go?" Nymie wondered and then a terrifying idea came into her mind. "Oh hell," she said and picked up the communicator.

"Rex, move the ship away from the tower, now," she yelled into it.

Rex jumped due to the sudden nature of the call. "What, why?" he asked in response. "Lexam cut off all the power but it's not electricity. That energy in the building has nowhere to go, we don't want to be here," Rex got the message, he was pretty sure Mocra would have prepared for a situation like that, but he trusted Nymie more than some rich CEO dumb enough to use Unicorn energy for anything in secret.

"Move the damn ship, clear us from the tower at least half a mile," he ordered the helmsman and in a panic the man frantically began to push buttons. Voltarice began to move away from the tower.

Rence was sitting at the top office in his tower when suddenly he noticed the ship was moving away. His office blocked telepathic messages coming or going, so he didn't understand why this was happening. He stood up and walked to the window overlooking the surface dwellings and noticed that all the lights that should have been on under the layer of fog, were not.

"What did you do?" Mocra yelled in anger and picked up his cell phone, it rang before he could make a call.

"What do you mean, what is going on?" he asked. "Sir, the sudden blackout has caused the power to surge. It's got nowhere to go and you need to leave the building immediately," the man on the other said in a panic. "What about the back up systems?" he asked in a hurry. "No good. The energy is screwing with everything, you need to leave, now," the man replied and hung up.

"Damn it," Mocra said and ran to his desk computer and quickly turned on the evacuation alarm. Then he walked to a body length mirror on his wall, waved his hand over it and it turned into a portal, he stepped into it and disappeared.

Chapter 15

Rex turned the ship around to face the tower, despite getting away in time, nothing seemed to be happening. He wondered for a moment if they had managed to contain the problem or if Nymie was just over reacting to it.

He and everyone near a viewing screen watched the tower, most of them wondering what was going on. For a few minutes nothing happened and Rex knew it had to be a false alarm.

Then the green tower exploded in a great, black and yellow mushroom shaped explosion of energy. "Oh, Taro," Rex said as his mind came back to him, he made his way to the intercom and started to talk.

"Brace yourself for impact, everyone, stabilizers on full power, shields at maximum," Rex ordered and clutched the sides of his chair. The whole ship rocked twenty seconds after the blast was seen and everyone held tight as the shields deflected the energy. Rex never closed his eyes despite how bright it was, he knew if he was seeing this in person he would have easily gone blind. Rex watched the smoke as it began to twist in the air.

"What?" Rex asked as he watched the whole explosion begin to spin.

He and everyone else could see that that this was turning into a massive portal. "So many unicorns were banished at once. I've never seen a reaction like this before," Evie said as she watched it. "I don't think anyone has," Boz replied and both of them were afraid.

The spinning came to an end and it looked as if a perfect circle of black energy had been torn out of the sky.

From the center of the black hole came a black ray of energy that flew in the ship's direction. Rex tried to order them to move but the blast was so fast that surrounded their ship in a second. Every system on the ship shorted out and the Voltarice was powerless.

It began to fall into the sea below them as the black surge of energy vanished into the distance. Everyone in the ship was left in darkness. The ship listed to the starboard side and crashed into the ocean, sinking beneath the waves and none of them could even get a distress signal out before the impact. The crew and hunters of the Voltarice were alone.

Drask woke up in the dark, something was on top of her but she couldn't tell what it was besides it being heavy and made out of metal. "Anyone alive?" she asked into the dark but no one responded. There were flashes of sparks raining down in the distance from something.

"What in the hell hit us?" she asked as she tried to move the thing on her but it was solid. "Anyone? I can't be the only one alive," she said to herself and lay there, it could have been hours after the attack or minutes. Time was impossible to measure in the dark and she didn't know how long she was out, either. Suddenly she heard footsteps coming in her direction.

"Hey, hey you, I need help can you see me?" she asked but there was no reply. "Come on now isn't the time for games," Drask weakly said to whoever was coming in her direction. "I see you," she said and seconds later Drask felt the extremely heavy thing holding her down be lifted up. The sudden movement sent waves of pain through her but she didn't cry out. The sparks revealed the outline of a woman.

"Who are you?" Drask asked as the being tossed the heavy object away with one arm. "I am Unie," she said and didn't worry about the pain or potential damage it would do as the machine pulled her off the ground. Drask winced again but managed to keep ahead of the emotions.

"How long ago were we attacked?" she asked the machine as she was carried. "It has been two hours since impact. My repair pod was undamaged, but I was in stasis to, stay out of the way. I have not seen anyone else. We are going to sick bay," the machine said and Drask widened her eyes. "No, I need to repair the engines, we can't leave," she replied. Drask wasn't sure if she could work at all in the dark, and the amount of pain she was in.

"Do not talk, you are bleeding. Focus on breathing and staying awake. I will do my best to get you out of here," the machine replied to her and they continued to move. Drask could see nothing and had to trust the machine completely. She could feel her blood running down her back, but since everything hurt she didn't know where the wound was. She wasn't too eager to look for it.

Tayne was in the middle flipping through a big thing of notes that meant nothing to him. Some kind of emergency going on but he didn't worry about it. A few minutes later, all of the sudden everything went black and shifted to the side. Tayne was smashed against the wall. The boxes weren't heavy but something sharp was inside one of them. It tore through the side and stabbed him in the stomach. "Oh, what the hell," he said with a groan, there wasn't any pain but the damage was enough to make him take notice.

He felt weaker already and knew he needed blood to regenerate himself. As far as he knew there was only one source available near him. First he had to make sure to pull whatever was impaling him out.

Nymie was smashed against the wall with so much force that her weight cracked the metal. She woke up and was confused. Everything was black and she didn't know how long she was out for. The last thing she remembered was reading about Albert Grayson when something rocked the boat. She slowly pushed herself up to her feet but the floor was weird. It was only seconds before she realized that she was standing on the wall and everything was on its side.

"This is not going according to plan," she said to herself and wondered why it was still dark, the emergency generators should have kicked in by now. If they weren't that meant the life support system was offline, too.

She walked towards where the door was supposed to be and grabbed the flashlight that was beside the door, turned it on. She looked around and saw that the place was a mess, but thankfully there wasn't any water leaking in.

"Nymie, are you over there?" Tayne asked as the light came on. "No, it's the Red Mirror. Who do you think it is?" she asked back and made her way over to him.

"I'm impaled by something. I could use your help," he replied and Nymie shined the light on to him and saw the blood. She put her hands on the box and pulled it off. "Weird, looks like a piece of a desk or something," she said and tossed the box into the dark.

"I hate to ask but, do you think I could get some blood from you, without it I'm, well, useless," Tayne said and Nymie looked around. "Fine, but if you tell anyone I did this I'll ash you without thinking about it," she replied and rolled up her sleeve and got to her knees. Tayne sunk his fangs into her green skin and closed his eyes. Nymie sighed, it felt like the warmth was being drained out of her at an alarming rate of speed.

"Okay, that's enough," she said and Tayne let go. "Sorry, trolls taste really good," he replied, already stronger than before. "Uh, thanks," Nymie replied and they both stood up, she helped him. "Come on, let's get out of here and find the others," she said and Tayne nodded in agreement.

Evie and Boz never made it to where they were supposed to go.

"Evie, are you alive?" Boz said into the darkness. They were going to the engine room, he wanted to check something but everything went to hell about halfway there.

They decided to walk and now they were in some hallway. Even with Boz's natural Elf eyesight, he couldn't see anything in here at all.

"I am alive, but something is wrong. All of the magic, the energy is gone," she said and continued. "I can feel it. Whatever hit this ship sucked the life, energy, everything right out of it. We are only alive because we are inside," she said weakly and coughed.

"Alright, we need to get you in some water because you won't last long without the star, there is an escape hatch a couple of junctions from here, we can get there," Boz replied into the dark.

"I think my leg is broken, I can't get out of here on my own," she replied through pain and Boz sighed. "Okay listen. You sound close, I am going to get a flashlight so we can see what we are doing and I'll try to get you out," he said to her and very carefully tried to stand up, feeling around slowly for anything that he might run into on accident.

"Just be careful, it's starting to hurt worse now, this really sucks," she said and Boz smiled because she wasn't panicking right now.

A few minutes later he found what he was looking for on the floor turned into a wall. He switched it on and swung around. Evie wasn't that far away from him and she was right, her leg was broken and a bone was sticking through the scales.

"I'm sorry, this is going to hurt. On the plus side you get to hold the flashlight," he said to her and smiled. She wasn't in the mood to smile. Boz got on his knees and came to the injury. He handed her the flashlight and placed his hands on the scaled leg.

"Think of something happy," Boz said and Evie barely registered the words as she took the light. With a swift snap the bone was set back into place.

Evie screamed in pain but Boz held her steady. "I know, it hurts, but you'll be okay," Boz said to her and noticed her clothes were gone without any magic to sustain them.

"If you tell anyone what you saw I'll put your mind into a jellyfish and you'll never say anything again," she said to him in a very clear, distinctive voice. "Don't worry. Doctor remember, anything I might see or touch I have to keep to myself, I'll find you something soon. Saving your life is my main worry right now," he said and carefully put his hands under her and lifted her up off the ground. Elroxians were naturally light, despite their skin being a little abrasive.

"I need something to wear, let's go to the storeroom and find something," she said to him and Boz rolled his eyes. "Yeah, wouldn't want anyone seeing you like this in a life and death situation, clearly this is the more important thing," Boz said and didn't want to carry her that far away but he also didn't want to be a jellyfish either. So, he decided that he was going to the storeroom.

Rex was on the bridge, the arms of his chair kept him from falling to the far wall but everyone else on the bridge had fallen out of theirs. The room was full of sparks, wires and smoke. The sparks were minimal, as if they were the last the ship had to offer.

Rex didn't dare move, it was a long drop down from where he was from here. It was a strange thing hanging in the darkness like this because it was almost felt like he was dead already.

"Hey, is anyone alive down there?" he yelled out into the darkness, but if there was, no one was responding to him. "Damn," he said and sitting here, all he could do was think about what it was that hit the ship and knocked it out of the sky with one hit. Nothing was coming to mind, he kept replaying the event over and over and he'd never seen anything like it.

A horrible feeling was coming up over and over again. All of this was his fault, he was the one who cut off the power and caused this overload. He couldn't even imagine how many people he was responsible for killing and should have known better.

A part of him knew that whatever came out of that portal had the potential to end the world as he knew it but wasn't sure why.

"Gods, if you're listening. I hope you don't hate me too much. I think I helped to unleash something that I don't quite understand. Maybe you can help me out a little bit, maybe you can show a little mercy on us so we can get it right or get the chance to make it right," Rex said to anyone who was listening, but there was no reply. No gods, no divine intervention, nothing.

"Okay, I guess I deserve that, but I am sorry," Rex said with a sigh. Suddenly from the wall above him a shower of sparks began to explode from the metal. Rex looked away as soon as he saw it. Within seconds a large, circular piece of metal sailed inches past his face.

"Hello in there, anyone alive?" a voice cried out into the dark. "I'm here, I don't know the status those below. Help them first," Rex cried out. "Sorry, Commander but we have orders to get you and your team out as soon as we can," the voice replied, closer this time as the light burned through the cut hole. "Alright, just be careful, one wrong move and I won't be going anywhere," Rex replied, still not seeing who it was. Then the voice was right next to him.

"Don't worry, sir, we're professionals," a dwarf said to him with a smile, and more importantly had another harness to pull Rex up.

"Lifeforms detected, trying penetrate the hull just ahead us," the machine said and Drask turned her head. It could have been anything from an enemy to a rescue team, she was hoping it was someone she knew, or friendly at least. "I'm in no condition to fight them so if you are, be ready," Drask replied weakly, feeling the life drain out of her as they walked.

"There is no reason to fight, they are wearing Emerald Watch badges, I believe it's a rescue team looking for survivors," she replied to her and kept on walking forward. Drask thought she saw sparks cutting through the wall in the distance, and that was the last thing she saw before passing out in the arms of the machine.

Unie didn't slow down or notice Drask's condition. She was programed to fix and maintain other machines, not living things. In the distance a sheet of metal fell forward, a man stepped in and shined their flashlight in her direction.

"I am in need of assistance, I am a utility bot, you should help me," she said and the man was stunned by the naked, blood covered woman standing in front of him. "I got one, I need a medic team now," he yelled back through the hole. Seconds later three others came running in with equipment. The machine held Drask out and the others took her away, laid her on the stretcher to get to work. The first man came back in and threw a blanket over Unie.

"I am not cold," the machine replied.

"No, but you are distracting. We'll find you something to wear on the rescue ship," the rescue worker replied and did his best to not look at her directly.

Nymie and Tayne were lost, she wished she paid more attention to things other than where the food and the bridge was. She was scared to death that she'd find a hallway turned into a death trap because a door was left open. Every step was made carefully, but there was another problem. The floor was wet, the water was leaking in from somewhere and the air was getting thinner.

Trolls needed more than the average race to function correctly due to their size and she was feeling the effects of the lack of air with each step she took. "Always thought I'd be eaten by a unicorn or something. This wasn't something I saw coming, fate is weird," she said to herself as she pressed forward, having no idea where she was going still. Each breath was getting harder to take. "Nymie, are you alright?" Tayne asked her.

"No, its pretty hard to breathe, I think I need to take a break," she replied and slumped against the wall. Tayne's red eyes widened. "It's the blood I took. Listen you stay here and I'll look for a way out," he said and walked past her. "Okay, sure, good plan," she replied.

Time passed by at a strange pace in the dark. Tayne left, what felt like hours ago now. Maybe it was only minutes, maybe hours. She lost track. It was obvious Tayne wasn't coming back in her addled mind so Nymie strained and pushed herself out of the sea water. Getting to her feet took more effort than she remembered it doing before. She gazed into the dark and started walking ahead, thinking nothing besides putting one foot in front of the other.

She was paying less attention to her surroundings and with the next step she fell into the deep, freezing water and disappeared. Immediately she realized her Aquarian star wasn't working in a panic. She swam back to the surface and grabbed the edge, out of breath.

"Maybe I should just get it over with, there isn't any way out of here," she said to herself and considered sinking below the waves for the last time. Her mind burned with negativity right now.

"You could, but that'd just be a waste of life and beauty," a voice said to her from the darkness. "What, who's there?" she replied to someone she couldn't see and didn't know.

"Give me your hand, I'll pull you up," the voice said to her and she shook her head. "I'm huge, there is no way you can pull me up, but thanks," she said and laughed about it. "Trust me, give me your hand. I'll pull you up," the voice said again and Nymie lifted her hand up, amused at the thought of too many people pulling her eight-foot frame out of the water.

Suddenly she felt the strongest grip she'd felt outside of a giant or one of her own kind take her hand and lift her straight up out of the water and back on to the wet metal wall on the other side of the pit.

"Who are you?" she asked, still not seeing anyone there.

"A friend who stopped by, look, the people you need to find are that way, there is a light at the end of the tunnel, its faint but you can see it. Follow it to safety," the voice said and after that there was a slight breeze, the smell of the ozone followed it. Nymie didn't know what was going on. She squinted her eyes and there it was at the end of the tunnel, a dim light.

"Thanks," she said, still out of breath but feeling better. Despite being in the water, she found that she was completely dry and also decided that now wasn't the time to question it.

Chapter 16

Boz and Evie made it into the storeroom, only to find it a complete disaster. Things were thrown everywhere and there was only so much you could see. "Well what are you waiting for, go in there and get me something to wear," she said and Boz looked at her. "You sure are demanding for someone I could just leave here to dry out and die," he replied and carefully set her down.

"I'm a tad unhappy, I get cranky when I get injured and lose all of my magic, I'm sure you can relate," she replied and Boz shook his head.

"I don't know how I am going to find anything in here but I will give it a shot. If I don't come back, I died," he said to her and stepped into the dark and hoped for the best.

"I am glad you decided to come on this trip," a voice said to her and she jumped a little. "Who's there, who are you?" she asked immediately and looked around. "Just a friend, don't worry I won't hurt you. It looks like you could use some help down here, maybe I can be of assistance?" the voice asked her.

"I don't know. Something took out all of our energy. Something bad happened, also my leg is broken too," she said, not feeling afraid of whoever this was.

"I'll help you out, just this once. Maybe twice if you're really nice," the voice said and she felt a hand come over where the bone was broken. She gasped in pain, but instead of pain she felt her leg mend back into place, not only that but her felt her energy return at the same time.

"Who are you? Tell me," she said but the second she felt back to normal, she no longer felt a presence around her. Just the smell of ozone surrounded her for a brief second.

"Thanks," she said as she stood up and continued. "Golt," she said and her staff appeared in her hand at once and her clothes reappeared on her body.

"Lumio," she shouted and a bright white light appeared from the top of her staff. Boz was revealed, looking through a pile of towels that he thought were clothes. "Hey, what's going on?" Boz asked and shielded his eyes at the sudden light that was way brighter than any flashlight.

"My energy came back, it doesn't take long for that to happen thankfully," she replied and walked towards him, a good healing spell and I am good as new, let's get out of here," she said to him and Boz nodded. "I am also sensing lots of life on the outside of this ship, rescue teams are coming in from all over the place. There isn't one too far away from us so let's go," she said and started to walk away. Boz climbed over the pile of junk to catch up with her in a hurry.

"Do you think we are the only ones alive?" Boz asked her. "No, we're not finished yet. We have to find out what is going on with whatever hit us," she replied to him and Boz could only hope she was right.

Nymie followed the light at the end of the tunnel and ran right into two rescue workers that were trying to cut through a door.

"Oh, you're alive, great. We left a marker trail to the exit, follow it please," a woman said to her. "Thanks, and thanks for coming to save us, oh, and the hallway is going to flood, there is a leak somewhere down that way," she replied, pointing into the black.

The worker just smiled, but quickly focused on what she was doing. Nymie walked around them and soon enough found herself facing an exit port. "I am so out of here," she said and didn't ask anyone permission to walk through it. The tunnel was much smaller than the ship she was in, she had to get to her hands and knees to make her way forward in the clear tunnel.

She was surrounded by black water and could only hope that her weight wasn't going to break this thing. She crawled up the tunnel, thankfully it didn't break and she came out the other end. Scaring the others who weren't expecting anyone to come out of the port tunnel.

"Hey, how's it going," she said to them and they were still catching their breath. "Why didn't you come through the evacuation tunnel?" one of them asked, confused. "I couldn't find it and got tired of waiting for someone to tell me where it was," she replied to them and looked around. This ship was much smaller than the Voltarice but she didn't mind. "The others are in the sick bay, one of your senior crew is being operated on right now and your robot refused to leave her side," the rescue worker said to her.

Nymie's eyes widened and she quickly walked off, three seconds later she came back.

"Where is the Sick bay on this boat?" she asked. "Second level, room six," she replied to her. Nymie nodded with a slight smile and walked off again in a hurry. Within minutes she found her way to the Sick bay and stood outside of it.

"Who is it?" she asked the machine who was now wearing a blue jumpsuit sitting on a bench close to the door. "It is the one you call Drask. Whatever force hit the ship not only took out all energy sources, it drained the energy from the body. They think the body cannot heal itself. They are doing all they can," Unie replied and Nymie sat next to her.

"Why are you okay?" she asked the robot. "I was in the repair pod at the time of the attack, the extra shielding protected me from whatever this was, that is my theory anyway," she replied to her. Nymie looked through the window and began to worry about her friend but didn't want to let her mind wander into the dark thoughts again. She would hope and wait for the results of whatever they were doing.

Rex walked into the sick bay viewing area later and was happy to see Nymie there but quickly decided that now was not the time to smile. Drask was still under the knife and he sat down beside Unie.

"We still don't know what did this, but a military outpost tracked the energy going out, deep into the Yalo ocean towards Calex Island," Rex said and Nymie shook her head.

"There isn't anything way out there beyond the wall but monsters and other vicious things that nobody thinks about," she replied to him. Neither one took their eyes off what they could see going on in the room, it wasn't much, there were too many people in the room. Rex nodded in agreement.

"Yes, and we are going there as soon as we can. So, I suggest you do your best to get some sleep if you can, I know this is going on but we are going to need everyone as well as they can be. Whoever did this Is going to pay for it," Rex said and narrowed his eyes.

"Any word from the others?" Nymie asked him.

"Boz and Evie are fine. Tayne is helping the rescue team recover the ones who lived," he said to her and sighed. "Alright, if anything happens just wake me up," she said, leaned back and closed her eyes. Rex didn't say anything, there was nowhere big enough for her to sleep comfortably anyway so here was as good as place as any for her to try and do it.

Evie and Boz sat in the ship's mess hall, or what passed for one on this ship. It was nothing compared to the Voltarice but it worked.

"Someone healed me," Evie finally admitted to Boz as she held her new Aquarian star in her right hand, and he raised an eyebrow.

"Who was this hero?" he asked back and Evie took a drink of her coffee and shook her head. "I don't know, it was a guy, I think. I never saw him. Not only did he heal me, he gave me back my energy too," she said and took another sip. "Well sounds like a good deal to me then," Boz replied, trying to keep his thoughts off of what happened to Drask and the ship, plus everyone else on it.

"I think it was Elrox," she said and Boz coughed as the theory caught him by surprise. "You think the God of the Sea showed up to help you, why?" he asked, not believing any of this. "No real reason, but it sure felt special," she said and smiled. "Well, whatever, all I know is I am glad you are okay," he replied to her and someone brought them their burgers, it was really the only thing on the menu.

"Thanks," Evie said and the server smiled, and he walked away. Boz looked out the window and saw that the sun was setting, it's been a very long day. "Let's eat and get some rest. I have a feeling we'll be moving again sooner than later," Evie said and took a bite.

"Yeah, but we'll need a new ship," Boz replied, he was missing the Voltarice already.

Chapter 17

Tayne didn't see it but he could feel the sun dropping out of the sky. Rummaging through the depths of the wrecked, increasingly waterlogged Voltarice he had only discovered fifteen living people on it. Everyone else so far was dead out of three hundred people. He did his best to not think about it.

"This is command, come in over," a voice came on the radio from the man behind him. "This is rescue five, what's going on," he replied. "The vampire is needed back on the command ship, relay the message," the voice said and Tayne turned around.

"I got the message," he said and started to walk away.

"Thanks for your help," the man said but Tayne was already gone. "Vampires creep me out," he said to himself before continuing the search. He could feel the sun going down, his powers were slowly returning to full strength. He was at the exit port in seconds and up the connection tunnel in about the same amount of time.

"Where's Rex?" Tayne asked the one who contacted him on the radio, who was still in the process in putting it back down. "God damn!" the man said as he jumped from his sudden appearance.

"Sick bay, and if you—" Tayne was already gone. "Never mind," he finished and tried to calm down.

Tayne walked into the sick bay and was glad to see Nymie was here, but sleeping and Rex looked at him. "Drask is not getting better and it's not looking good. The only one who can save her, is you," he said to him and Tayne looked through the window. "We aren't supposed to turn people who aren't willing," he replied to him.

"She's going to die, I can feel it. We either act now or sit back and watch. Her body is shut down, they can't save her because something literally drained her. I'm not asking you to turn her, I'm asking for a few drops of blood. A jumpstart," Rex said and Tayne looked into the room.

"It could save her. It could destroy her mind," he replied and continued, "but I'll try to do it if you really want me too," he said and walked towards the door. "I'd rather try this than just watch her die like on some table without putting up a fight," he said and Tayne nodded.

"Sounds good to me, be right back," he said, walked to and opened the door.

"You can't be in here," one of the doctors said and Tayne easily pushed him out of the way and walked over Drask's body. He pulled a small knife out of his jacket and quickly sliced his hand open. He held his bleeding hand over Drask's wounds and bled into them.

"Stop, you'll kill her," another doctor screamed out but it was already done, his hand was already healed. Ten seconds passed and Drask didn't change at all. Then, before his eyes the horrible wounds the doctors made and the ones she suffered began to close. He took a step back and waited.

"What, where am I?" she asked weakly and opened her eyes.

"You're going to be alright I think. But you were going to die so I had to give you some of my blood so you could be, well, restarted, it was the only way," Tayne said to her and Drask was feeling better but furious.

"You mean I have your toxic blood in me, really, what gave you the right to do that? I was better off dead," she said angrily and started to pull the wires off of her body. "I guess we will never know, don't worry. It was just enough to jump start you, you won't turn but I'd avoid any direct sunlight for a few days. Whatever hit us drained the energy out of everything it touched. The ship is dead, I was drained and not many people made it. We are going to, I assume, find out what it was," Tayne said and didn't bother to look away as she pulled off the coverings the doctors put on her.

"Where in the hell are my clothes?" she asked, looking around. "How would I know, I just got here," he replied and looked around but didn't see anything. Then he looked at the doctor who was standing in the corner, then looked at Drask, then back to the doctor.

"You, where did you put the clothes?" she asked and the doctor shook his head. "We had to cut them off, they were soaked with blood, you wouldn't want them," he said and walked over to the opposite door, opened it and reached inside to pull out a long white lab coat like thing. He tossed it to her and she quickly put it on. It was just a little too big but she didn't mind.

"Thank you for doing everything you could to try and save me," she said to him as she stood up. "Just, we don't know what the long term effects of vampire blood are, without tests it's completely different for each person. Take it slow," the doctor said as she walked out, he had no idea if she listened or not.

Rex, the robot and a still sleeping Nymie were still sitting there. "Welcome back to the land of the living," Rex said to her and Drask shook her head. "I don't know how alive I am going to be with vamp blood in me but I guess time will tell how all that turns out," she said and smiled, she liked it that they were here. "You'll be fine, it was my idea anyway. Tayne didn't want to do it but I knew we didn't have an option, so here we are," he replied to her. She glared at him and he could only smile.

"Hey, at least he didn't bite me I guess. I didn't want to be a vampire. I enjoy life a little too much for a strictly liquid diet," Drask replied and for a minute it was as if nothing had happened at all in their lives to get them here, but reality set back in a hurry. "It doesn't work that way but, never mind," Tayne said and decided to not get into the details of it.

"So, they tracked the, whatever it was, making a very straight line straight to Calex island and that is where we will be going next," Rex informed them all. "We have a ship on its way to meet us, it's not the Voltarice but it will do so I suggest you get some rest and make sure that you're up to the challenge because it will be one. We have about four hours to kill and make sure to pick up a working Aquarian Star, too," Rex said to them all.

"Alright, what did I miss?" Nymie asked as she woke up and then she saw Drask. "Hey, you're alive, great," she added with a sleepy smile and a yawn. "Yeah, just let us know when the ship gets here. I am going to get some rest," Drask said and walked out, and the rest of them slowly stood up and started to walk out. The robot remained there.

"Come on metal girl, you don't need to sit here by yourself," Tayne said to her. The machine looked at him, stood up and followed him out of the room. "You can stay up with me, I guess," he finished and laughed a little bit.

Four hours passed by and soon enough another, lesser ship had met up with the rescue vessel.

Rex was already on the bridge and getting used to the second-rate transport, but it was better than nothing. "Is everyone aboard that needs to be aboard?" he asked into the intercom. Not interested at all in protocol.

"I guess the Commander has had it," Evie said to herself, reached over and flipped her signal switch to the bridge to indicate she was on board. Rex watched one by one as the lights flipped from red to green. If anyone wasn't on board that needed to be he would deal with that problem later, but according to this everyone was here.

"Good, we are leaving, it'll just be us. I'll be driving the ship to Calex island. We will be there just before the sun comes up. Be ready for anything," he said. Through the viewing screen he could see that the black tear in the sky had disappeared. Whatever its purpose was, had been finished.

Chapter 18

The trip to Calex Island was surprisingly, uneventful.

Soon enough, he island loomed in the darkness before the ship. In the night, black ocean and with stars behind it, it was hard to see.

"We should wait until the sun comes up before we go venturing on to the island," Drask said as they all stood on the upper deck, looking towards the place. "That's the best thing I've heard all night," Nymie added but Tayne shook his head.

"What if whatever is on that island is doing some stupid ritual and by the time we get there it will be too late," he said to them. Evie stared at the island.

"You know, are we really sure it didn't just sail on past here? I'm not sensing anything out here besides a couple of weak auras, but nothing seriously horrible," she said and shrugged.

"I agree. I do not detect anything," Unie said and she gazed into the dark.

"Well outside of here it could have gone anywhere. We have to at least give it a look to make sure. Wouldn't it be funny if we decided to not go look and we doomed the world because it was hiding here? Yeah, that's exactly what I want to be remembered for, the guy who said to not check," Rex said and looked to the stars in the sky.

"It'll be lighter in an hour, get ready to go. Take only what you need," he said and walked away from them.

"I hope it's a nice place. I hear good things about it, hardly anyone ever comes back," Nymie said and laughed. "How is that good?" Drask asked her quickly. "Well, it means that people come back, so there is a chance that we won't just disappear here, not without a fight at least," she replied and Boz nodded.

"Don't worry, I won't let anything happen to you," Boz said to her without really thinking about it. "Oh, you're going to protect me, well, great," she said and put her hand on the top of his head and rubbed his golden hair. Drask laughed and Tayne just rolled his red eyes.

"Boz and Nymie, a couple, I'll believe that when I see it, but be careful, Boz. I heard that Trolls like to eat Elves," he said with a laugh. Nymie immediately reached over and hit the vampire in the back of the head so hard that he fell off the side of the ship. "And that's for abandoning me back on the Voltarice," she said mostly to herself.

"We don't eat elves, at least not anymore," she said as she looked over the edge. "You should have hit him harder," Drask commented as Boz got closer to Nymie.

"He's a vampire, he'll be fine. We've talked long enough, let's get ready to go," she replied, turned around to go back inside the ship. "Enjoy the climb back up, you snozbucket," Boz said over the edge, feeling confident Nymie at least was going to be there for him.

The others followed Nymie back inside.

Tayne was already clawing his way back up the side of the ship when a hand appeared to help him up. It was the robot. "I will help you," she said to him. Tayne took her hand and was pulled up with ease. "Thanks," he said to her, the robot only smiled in response. "You are a vampire, how come you didn't just fly back up?" Unie asked him. "Well, flight takes a lot of energy, and I managed to catch the metal before I needed to fly. Scratched the paint job up pretty good but I think they'll understand," he replied.

"Good, let's prepare for the expedition," Unie said. Tayne looked at her. "You don't need to come with us if you don't want to," he replied.

"The suspect controlled me, made my actions responsible for killing everyone I was supposed to help. It is my duty to, as you would call it, get some payback," she replied to him. Tayne wondered just how advanced Unie really was. "I understand, let's go," he replied and the two of them walked inside.

"Is everyone ready to go?" Rex asked and they were all in their individual transport speeders in the docking bay of the ship, floating on the water. "Let's get this over with already so I can go home, I want to know how the trial turns out," Drask said and Rex had completely forgotten about that. The others were as ready as they were ever going to be.

"Let's go," he said and his shield activated along with the rest of theirs. Rex activated his speeder and sank under the water with the rest of them.

Together they quietly made their way to Calex Island through the dark water with nothing but their computers to guide them and allowing them to see through the black.

There wasn't anything to see however, all of the normal life in the sea around this place appeared to be long gone, as if some predator was stalking the sea that was invisible to everything and everyone. Despite the weirdness of the situation, nothing attacked them.

They broke the surface of the sea and pulled on to the beach, digging into the wet sand. The only sound around them was the crashing waves. They all got out and Evie looked around.

"Strange," she said and walked over to a tree. There was a symbol carved into it, she scraped an extra line into the bottom of it and it began to glow bright green, then it faded away.

"No wonder this place didn't have anything coming off of it, it was warded," she said to them and turned around. With one of the wards broken the others on the trees began to glow green as well, the ward circle had been broken. "I hate wards, who would take the time to protect a whole island?" Drask asked.

"Someone who really didn't want to be found, obviously," Boz replied to her.

"Well, great, now we know we are on to something, let's keep going," Tayne said to them and unattached his shotgun from its holster at his side. "Yeah, get your weapons out, we don't know what is in here," Rex said to them and they all followed the vampire's lead.

They began walking through the trees but being unfamiliar with the place and it still being dark out it was hard to see anything before it became a problem. Tayne and Boz were having the easiest time navigating the thick jungle with the strange plants so they were leading the charge into the interior of the island. Suddenly the faint smell of smoke and glow of fire could be seen in the distance through the trees ahead of them.

The group moved to the edge of the trees and saw a clearing before them and they all became nervous. There was a large fire burning in the middle of a circle of various, low level unicorns, bowing their heads to a man in bright red and black robes. He was screaming something in a language they didn't understand and looking up at something. Rex and the others looked up at the sky and there were no stars above them.

It was a swirling black mass of silent energy.

"Why didn't we see that from the boat? That looks like something that would be kind of hard to miss," Boz said almost too loud. "I don't know but look at all the horns, they are acting very strange. Do you think it's the Black Unicorn?" Nymie asked them and Rex, nor anyone else knew. "I would assume yes," Tayne replied.

"We need to do something, what's the plan?" Tayne asked them and it was clear that no one had an actual plan. "I can hit the mage from here, maybe the shock will knock the unicorns out of their trance and they'll tear him apart," Drask suggested and continued, "then we can take the unicorns out like we normally do," she finished.

"There is a seventy five percent chance that the mage will be unaffected by the blast and our position will be revealed by this action resulting in a one hundred percent death rate," Unie said to them and Rex rolled his eyes.

"I still don't know why we brought the pessimistic robot along," Rex whispered to himself.

"Do we have any other ideas or is this the only one we have to try?" Rex asked them and no one seemed to have any better plan then to go in guns blazing and hope for the best. "Okay then, let's do it," Rex said to them and they began to spread out to surround the strange ritual that was going on in front of them.

Drask took careful aim at the mage's head and waited until the others were where they needed to be for the best chance to take out the monsters surrounding the red mage. Rex nodded to Drask from a distance and she fired. A bright green bolt of energy fired from the weapon. The person in the red robes was struck in the back of the head, and fell to the ground.

The unicorns, however, didn't even move.

"Well that's new," she said and was at a loss as to what do next, all the others were too. Whatever was above them had a hold on the monsters unlike anything they had ever seen before, it was clearly not the mage in red who was doing this.

"That really hurt you know," the mage said out loud and began to stand back up. "You can come out now. I knew you were coming. I saw that ship hours ago so you really need to work on your stealth skills," the person said but didn't turn around. One by one the hunters began to come out of the woods. "Okay, you got us, but what is all of this. Why are these monsters just waiting?" Rex asked, blaster in hand as he did. The mage took the hood down and it turned out to be a woman, not who they were expecting.

"Monsters, no, these are the children of the Abyss, you see, this world Is actually theirs and people like you keep sending them away, but all that is about to change," she said and smiled. "Abyss, I don't even know what that means but nothing is going to change. These monsters are going back to where they came from," Nymie said and raised her axe to cut the horn off of a Geo horn she was close to.

"They came from here, this is their world, not ours. I am bringing them home and the greatest one of them all, the Black Unicorn, he will arrive and go into the chosen vessel to bring in a great new age. Or, I guess back to the way things used to be before the Gods showed up and ruined everything," she said and pushed the black hair out of her purple eyes.

"Well, true or not we have to keep things the way they are," Boz said as Nymie brought the axe down and cut off the stone horn of the Geo horn. The beast screamed, and as expected its body collapsed into the dirt, crumbling away into nothing. None of the others reacted, but seconds later a thin beam of white energy came down from the black mass to where the pile of dirt lay and entered it. The monster quickly reformed into the monster it was and Nymie jumped back.

"What in the hell is this," she said and the mage just laughed. "See, I allowed you to be here because there is nothing you can do. You know that unicorns can only be banished, but they always return. What do you think is above us now? Just some odd cloud that I decided to summon, really?" she asked her and laughed again. "So that is where they come from, the other side of that energy," Tayne looked up and figured this mage was telling the truth, maybe about everything.

"So, Rex, yes, I know your name, all of us do, what do you intend to do now?" she asked him and Rex thought about it for a minute. "Well, I suppose I am just going to arrest you and bring you back to the capital for questioning. I have a feeling these unicorns aren't here for you and have no reason to protect you. Whatever is coming down has their attention. That seems like a plan to me," he replied to her and her eyes narrowed.

"You can't do that, I am the conduit, none of you can touch me," she replied and clapped her hands. Immediately a wave of deep purple fire spread out in all directions from them and everyone dived back into the trees to get out then the mage started to run.

"Don't let her get away," Rex said and Evie pointed her staff at the mage's feet, the earth itself rose up and surrounded the mage's feet at once, bringing her to the ground. Boz just looked at him. "Did you really just say that?" he asked in disbelief. "Yeah, sorry," Rex replied and smiled.

"Maybe you should do that first before the crazy one gets a chance to fry all of us," Boz said as he picked himself off the ground as the others did. "Sorry, I was too busy trying to figure out why we aren't dead yet," she said and couldn't take her eyes off of the swirling mass above them.

"You can't take me away, the ritual isn't done, and we'll all be destroyed if it's not completed, don't you understand, we are all going to die," the mage was screaming, trying to get away. Tayne walked up to her and with ease put her hands behind her back to cuff her with special anti-magic metal cuffs. As soon as he did that he pulled her out of the ground and to her feet.

"We can't leave these monsters here like this, they won't stay here like this forever," Nymie said as she looked, still amazed by the circle of horror that surrounded her and fighting every urge to start trying to banish them as fast as she could.

"For now, there isn't anything we can do, you saw what happened, but I think we should get out of here just in case the trance breaks and we end up getting eaten," Rex said and started to walk away. The rest of them started to follow him. "I am telling you people, if I don't finish there will be no controlling what happens next. We will all die. I had a plan you know. We knew what we were doing. Why are you messing everything up?" she started to scream and fight to get away when Tayne just punched her and knocked her out.

"It's what we do," he said and threw the mage over his shoulder.

"Let's get out of here," Evie said not approving of how he chose to take care of the situation but now wasn't the time to argue about it. With the rising sun it was much easier to get through the twisted jungle, luckily, they didn't see any hostile lifeforms, likely due to the strange magic that was taking place there. The speeders were just where they left them.

"Let the mage go with the robot so in case she wakes up she can't take any of us hostage or something stupid like that," Rex said and Tayne gave him a funny look for a second but quickly handed the unconscious woman off to the machine, who easily carried her to the transport and set her inside.

"Is it just me or is that thing in the sky getting bigger?" Drask asked and looked up at the black thing above them. "No, it is. I don't know why but we need to get away from it, you do remember what it did last time, right?" Rex reminded them and that was more than enough encouragement for them to get in their transports and make their way back to the ship.

Chapter 19

The mage woke up in a bleak, small metal room sitting in a chair and her wrists chained to a table. Across from her Rex was sitting there. "Hey, welcome back. Sorry for that but you were getting hysterical so we had to take care of it," he said and she shook her head, trying to get rid of the pain.

"You have to let me go or else you're all going to die, me too, all of us," she said to him in a hurry and Rex smiled. "Now explain to me why we are all going to die, I mean, details?" he asked her and she laughed at him.

"Fine, what do I care. When the blades were released in the north it started a chain of events. Prophecies you know? Albert and I, we dabbled in Unicorn mythology and legends, but he caught onto a story. Once the blades are opened, the unicorn shall return and the black veil will cover the whole of the world," she said and laughed, but continued, "Unicorn scholars always talked about the idea of a black unicorn and how it was able to control all the others," she said and Rex shook his head.

"I know about the theories, but I've faced these things for a long time. They've never even shown the slightest interest in working together, in fact they are so driven by keeping what's theirs they will banish their own kind most of the time, they are very anti-social," Rex responded to her and the mage just smiled.

"I know, but you saw it, there wasn't much killing going on in that circle. They were in communication with their leader, their, for all intense and purposes, God," she replied to him and continued. "Albert and I, we discovered how to potentially control the black unicorn. The ritual, the spell, we found it all. We hacked into the deepest magical vaults of information kept by the orders to find it. Albert was a genius like that and we found out that the power of the god needed a vessel to give up their own life," she said, that smile never left and those black eyes never blinked.

"Albert killed himself at work, I took his body. It's on that island. It's going to take the power of the God the only difference is I won't be there to bind it to my will so it'll be free to do what it wants, and all it wants is to scrub the world clean of everything that isn't part of its race," she said and laughed about it some more, clearly all of dark work had eroded her sanity in some crucial places.

"And what was your plan, what did you plan to do with all that power?" Rex asked her, he was pretty sure he knew the answer to this. "Me, no, the mind of the god would have been bound to me suppressed, but the power would be inside Albert. We were going to use it to destroy the Necromancer Delrax cult once and for all. They killed our families years ago in a raid in the out waters and we couldn't do anything. Nothing at all. Now we can, but you ruined it. Now the God will destroy us all. I guess in a roundabout way I'll get what I want. I just won't get to enjoy it as much," she said and put her face into her hands.

"Revenge, you didn't go to the Emerald Watch or anything?" Rex asked and she shot a glare of hate at him that made him jump back slightly in surprise. "Of course we did, we went to everyone we thought could help but the Delrax sect is very hard to find. Nothing was done. Nothing was ever done. After we were old enough, we took matters into our own hands and did the only thing that would promise us to get what we deserved," she replied to him and Rex shook his head.

"We can't do anything about any of that now. That had to be twenty-five years ago or more. Most of those people are likely dead by now anyway. Listen, we need a way to shut this madness down. Is there any way to banish the energy back to its own world," Rex tried to appeal to common sense. "Yes, but I'm not telling you what that method is. We've worked too hard for this sacrificed so much," she said and Rex shot her a glare.

"You mean you wiped out a whole village of innocent people for your revenge, is that the sacrifice you talked about?" Rex was angry but doing his best not to show it.

"We needed the souls, the souls are powerful you know. Strong enough to call the energy of the god to where we needed it to be, it was part of the prophecy for a reason, a cryptic message to tell people how to control the power," she replied to him and looked down. "Well alright, if you won't tell me I'll just have to get what I need another way. But I'll make sure you live to pay for what you did. Don't you even worry about that," Rex said and stood up to leave the room.

"Could I have some water?" she asked him.

"No," he replied before leaving the room and closing the door behind him.

"The energy over the island is only getting bigger," Evie said the obvious, everyone could see it and its bright yellow electric discharges that didn't quite look like lightning. "Yeah but is there an off switch? Is there anything we can do about it, the crazy in the room down the hall seems to think she's the only one who can do anything about any of this, she might be right," Rex replied and looked into the heart of the magical storm.

Something about it, besides being a supernatural event, seemed wrong. He'd seen mage storms before and weathered more than his fair share of them. This was not like any of those.

"Regardless of what we do I've already sent a warning back to the kingdom and told them what was going on, or at least what we think is going on," Tayne said to them. "Aw, look at you, you do have a heart after all. I didn't even have to tell you to do it," Rex replied and Tayne rolled his eyes. "Why don't we just let the crazy mage finish the ritual, at least then we can have some kind of control of the situation," Drask said to them and Rex considered it for a few seconds.

"Yeah, but she's going to kill a lot of people anyway and I don't see that working out very well for us either because, well, revenge never stops, there is always someone to blame," Rex replied and Drask shrugged. "Well can we contain this energy, shield the whole island maybe?" Nymie asked and that was a good idea, Rex smiled.

"We can try to do that, what do you think Evie?" he asked her and the mage looked at the growing storm. "We can try but it's going to take all the magic that I have in me to try to make this a thing," she said and tightened the grip on her staff.

"Well, we don't have much of a choice because, wait, I think we can have some help. The Delrax necromancer said to call them if we needed some help, I think this qualifies as needing some help," Rex said and picked up the communicator.

"You think, you actually want to trust some necromancers with this. There is enough magical energy building up here to power any group of mages for hundreds of years if they can tap it. Necromancers aren't exactly known for their trustworthiness," Boz said, all of this was making him uncomfortable as it was but calling them was just getting to be too much.

"We don't have a choice," Rex replied to him and began to dial. "Okay, but I still don't like it," Boz said and Nymie smiled. "Don't worry little guy, I'll protect you from the bad necromancers" she said and Boz smiled. "Thanks, I hope I won't need it," he replied in a much more serious tone.

Rex pushed the button on the communicator.

"Hi, remember me, Rex, we met the other day and we have a situation over Calex Island. Someone did something very bad and we are going to try and contain it but we need some more magical power than we have so can you send like, three or four of your people to my location so we can take care of this," Rex said and waited.

"We will send what you need, please stand by," a raspy voice replied.

"Yeah, cool. No one else is out here, you won't miss us. Just don't teleport into the water, that wouldn't look good and we'd make fun of you forever for it," Rex replied and cut off the communication. "See, I knew they'd help. They aren't all bad just mostly bad," he finished and now all he could do is wait for them to show up and hope for the best.

"I still don't like this idea," Tayne said what they were all thinking.

Minutes later there was a column of smoke on the bridge of their ship. One necromancer in a traditional black cloak. "Wait, your people only sent one, don't you think you'll need more than just one to help," Evie said, shocked they would be so arrogant.

"Sister, one is all we are going to need. I know some tricks they don't teach in that moldy school you went to," she said and removed her hood. She looked like any normal person, no dead skin or obvious contamination most of them had. The necromancer turned to look at the energy in the sky and smiled. "Wow, that could be entirely useful for all the experiments I want to do," she said and smiled.

"No, we need to contain the mess and make sure it can't ever get out," Evie said and the others were tense, weapons were close. "Yeah, I suppose you're right," the necromancer replied and walked toward the viewing screen. "We're going to need a cell phone for this. The old timers used crystals to bind and banish nasty things. I'll show you something you're never going to forget but I am assuming you're at least above the fourth rank in whatever you call your mage system these days?" she asked Evie, who scowled in returned.

"I'm qualified to do whatever it is you need help with, don't worry about it. Let's just get it done," she replied, the necromancer smirked and began to walk-out of the bridge and Evie followed. "Well that was fun," Nymie said as they left.

"Yeah, let's hope we don't die in the process of whatever happens next," Boz said and Rex kept his eyes on the viewing screen to watch what was going to come next.

Evie and the Necromancer stood side by side on the deck.

"Now, as I said the old ones used crystals, lots of crystals. Now days all we need is a cell phone, give me yours," she said to Evie and she pulled her thin white rectangle phone and handed it to her.

"Okay, this might not work and it will take all of our energy to contain something this big," she said and began to mystically carve a rune Evie didn't know on the back of the phone with her finger with blue lines of energy.

"Stop looking so confused, I got this," she said and finished. "Okay, what happens next is unpredictable but I think we can handle it," she said and Evie shook her head.

"What's your name?" Evie asked her. "I am Calibri, what difference does it make to you, let's get this over with so I can get home," she replied to her and held the phone up into the direction of the swirling mass. "Hold on to this thing so we can get this done. Focus all your energy into the phone, I will do the same and guide the sealing spell. If you hold anything back it won't work so now isn't the time to be worried about silly misgivings that make you paranoid about working with me," Calibri said and to her and Evie put her hand on the phone and together they held it up.

"Nou mare nou antre nan anile a p'ap janm fini an pou tout tan. Se pou tan kenbe ou e pa gen je janm jwenn ou," Calibri said with a surprising amount of authority that Evie thought she had and the phone began to glow.

"Say it with me, I know you don't understand the words but say it with me and we'll be okay," Calibri shouted to Evie and the mage nodded. Together they screamed the spell and the winds around them picked up, violently and the waves began to rock the ship as the intense power gathered around them.

Evie had never had to do a binding spell on this scale before, she didn't know what to expect and the waves were breaking her concentration.

"Last warning, fish girl, if you break concentration we will all die here, focus everything you have, now," Calibri screamed at her over the howling winds and waves. Evie narrowed her eyes and retained her focus on the work at hand.

"Nou mare nou antre nan anile a p'ap janm fini an pou tout tan. Se pou tan kenbe ou e pa gen je janm jwenn ou," they said together as loud as they could and the phone turned energy conduit glowed bright purple and fired a beam of light towards the energy in the sky and the island.

Everyone watched as half way to the target spread out in all directions to cover everything they could see. There was the sound of thunder and the shockwave of an invisible explosion that knocked the both of them to the deck of the ship. The vessel itself threatened to capsize with the shockwave.

"Are we still alive?" Evie asked as she struggled to get the ringing out of her head. "Yeah, but you're going to need a new phone," Calibri replied to her and handed her the burned, broken remains of her phone. "Well, I suppose it was worth it, I think we won," Evie said and struggled to stand up. Calibri had no trouble standing. The two of them looked out and all they saw was empty ocean before them. There was no sign of any island, or that one had ever been there.

"That's how the big binding circles work, if they work it and everything in the target zone is not only sealed, but hidden, as long as the magic remains intact anyway. No one but us knows it's here. We are in no danger of anyone breaking it open," she said and Evie immediately knew this was going to be leverage for the necromancers someday but didn't bother to mention it.

"Thank you for your help," Evie said and Calibri smiled. "No problem, it's always fun to work with a mainstreamer once and awhile. We're not all bad you know. We all have our issues but most of us are not too much different than you, we just took a different path. I hope you remember that," she said and looked away from the sea.

"Before you go, do you want to tell our crazy prisoner we just ruined all of her plans?" Evie asked and Calibri shrugged. "Alright, why not?" she said and the two of them walked off the deck.

The two of them walked through the ship and into the holding room. She was still there, the second Calibri walked in she tried to stand up and lunge forward in anger.

"You brought a Necromancer in my sight to what, torment me a little more," she said as the chains pulled her back down. "No. I came to show you that not all of them are bad and we just banished your energy and the rest of plan along with it, locked it up so no one will ever find it again," Evie said to her and crossed her arms. The chained mage just started to laugh.

"Let me guess, you bound the power and the island too, everything and you never got rid of the vessel," she said and kept laughing. "Vessel, what is she talking about, no one ever mentioned any vessel," Calibri said and looked at her. "I don't know, you got me. No one told me about it either," Evie said but wasn't too concerned about it.

"It doesn't matter if you bound it, you can't bind the power of a god. The process will complete in this world or any other. It cannot be stopped. You idiots didn't remove the vessel and it might take a little longer but you're still all going to die with me," she said and couldn't help herself but smile.

"That information would have been useful about ten minutes ago," Calibri said and was disappointed in this turn of events. "Well we need to break the spell and go in and get the body, we need to do this and-" Calibri cut her off. "Neither of us have any energy to do that right now, also, this lady is obviously a renegade mage, likely insane, we can safely assume that we won. Let's get out of here," she said and Evie wasn't really convinced of that but it was either believe the necromancer or the revenge consumed renegade.

She decided to go with the necromancer, turned towards the door and walked out. Calibri looked at the mage one last time before she followed Evie out of the room and closed the door behind her.

"So, you're sure that she's just crazy," Evie said as they walked towards the bridge.

"I don't know but if you would have shown fear in there that would have put her in control of the situation. I couldn't allow that. The only one I want controlling you in any situation is me," Calibri said to her and smiled, continuing, "everything I've magically bound, none of it has ever been found let alone escaped on their own, you need to trust me on this one. We can go back to killing one another tomorrow, but tonight we should celebrate on a victory," she said as they made it to the bridge Evie opened the door.

"We can go home," Evie said and a wave of exhaustion came over her, she was dehydrated and drained. "But for now I need to go to my room. I need to recover," Evie said and almost fell over. Tayne rushed to her side in a second and caught her.

"I got you," he said and picked her up, walking right back out from the bridge. "I'm tired too. If I rest here, do you promise you won't kill me?" Calibri asked them and Rex nodded.

"We won't kill you," he replied to her and she smiled, turned and walked out. "Nymie, set a course for home, we are out of here," Rex said to her and she smiled.

"I can't wait to get the hell home, not that I don't like you or anything, but I'm tired of this crap," she said and started to set the course for home.

Chapter 20

"All in all, it wasn't that bad of a trip. We all almost died twice but hey, that was worth it right. No horrible unicorn experiences, not a single serious necromancer attack. No ghouls. Nothing. I've had worse trips," Boz said to himself and turned on the television in the rec room. No one was transmitting anything, there wasn't an even a stand by message.

"Power must still be out back home," he said and shut the television off and sighed. There wasn't much to do for a medical officer on the trip home. The door behind him opened and he turned around. Nymie walked in. "We still have a date to finish, don't we?" she asked him and sat down beside him after moving the table out on the slide it was on.

"I didn't think it was a date but sure if that's what you want to call it," he said to her and laughed a little bit. "Did you know that Geo horn back on the island was the first one outside of training I've ever seen?" she asked him. "No way, that doesn't even seem possible," he responded and she smiled. "It's always an Electro horn or if I'm really unlucky a Blood horn," she said and Boz shook his head.

"Neither one sound very fun to me, how do you handle it," Boz was curious, he hated dealing with those things. "I beat them up until they die, that is my always, never fail plan," she said and laughed and Boz rolled his eyes. "Sure it is, sure, anyway. We don't get together much so I was wondering what you plan to do after you get back home," Boz said and Nymie could only smile.

The ship traveled through the rest of the day, the sun was beginning to set when it reached the Yalo wall. "Home sweet home," Rex said with a smile.

"This is the, um…Voltarice two, I guess, is there anyone there?" Rex asked after he turned the communication panel from his chair on. There was no response. "Weird, the generators should still keep the official channels open. What's going on?" he asked to himself and tried again, but once again there was no answer.

They were still too far away to see their home for right now but be was beginning to get worried that something horrible had actually happened here at home while they were away.

"Drask, how's our communication, is anything wrong with our systems?" Rex asked into the intercom. "No, nothing that I can tell on this end but it's funny. I'm not detecting any signals from the surface dwellers either. It's like everything has disappeared," she replied to him and Rex sighed.

"Thanks, keep trying to find someone and let me know when you do," Rex said and sighed keeping his eyes on the viewing screen. He trusted all the sensors on the ship but he always liked to see things for himself, he would make his way to the deck once they got closer.

Evie was sleeping in her water chamber, and she was in the grip of a terrible nightmare. She stood in the streets of the surface capital, everything was on fire. "This is going on now, it's no dream," Elrox said, standing behind her. "What caused this, why, what happened?" Evie had many questions but the God stood next to her. "It's your fault, but really you can't do anything about that now," he replied to her, but smiled.

"Listen, you need to hurry up, it's not going to last much longer. Actually, it's not going to last more than three hours, you can make it. I have faith in you." Elrox said to her. Evie could feel his warmth. She turned around to look at him, but was greeted with the decaying face of a Flesh unicorn's gnashing teeth. Evie woke up with a start and swam towards the intercom. "Rex, are you there?" she said out of breath. "Yeah I'm here what's up," he replied.

"You need to put full power to the engines. Everything on the surface of the Western Kingdom is under attack, you need to believe me, just do it," Evie screamed into the intercom. "Understood, get to the bridge as soon as you can and fill me in on the rest," Rex replied to her. Evie quickly casted her clothing spell with what little energy she had recovered and made her way through the airlock and into the hall. She used her staff as support to make her way down the hall. Luckily for her it wasn't that far away.

The doors slid open and Rex was there to meet her. "I've already given the order, what is the problem," he asked her and she caught her breath.

"Unicorns have invaded. I saw it in a dream, it's happening right now," she said and he narrowed his eyes. "Elrox himself was there, I have to believe it's true, please we have to hurry," she said and was so distraught that she almost collapsed, he caught her before she could hit the ground. "You go sit down, we are going as fast as this bucket can go," Rex said and helped her to an empty chair. Evie almost fell into it.

"Rest easy, we'll do what we can, and I hope you're not right," Rex said and worried about what they were going to find. Rex almost wanted to say something negative about the God of the sea, however, he also didn't feel like being turned into sea salt or something so he kept his mouth shut.

Rex kept this information to himself. He didn't see any reason to alarm anyone over what amounted to what could be a fever dream. But still the lack of signal from the city worried him more the longer it went and nothing was detected. He still could see nothing when Drask called him back on the intercom.

"You're not going to like this even a little bit. I tuned into a police scanner and apparently, it's insane out there. I've got reports that unicorns have, well, invaded the city, it's a blood bath," Drask said and Rex was confused how this could happen.

"How are the hunters doing?" Rex asked, worried about the rest of them.

"No mention of them was made. I can only assume they are in the mess or soon will be," she replied to him and Rex didn't know what he could do. "If you can get us their faster," Rex said into the intercom. "No need to worry, I'm pushing this pile as far as it can go. It's times like this I miss the Voltarice," she replied to him as she watched the gauge hit the red lines on her console. Rex didn't bother to reply.

They traveled through the air over the dark sea as fast as those second-rate engines could take them. Evie sat in that chair, still drained but aware of what was going on. Rex stood up from his chair as their ship began to approach what looked like a bank of fog in the distance.

It only took a few seconds to realize that there was more than just mist in this haze. The ash particles began to appear on the screen and he immediately knew it was smoke, they had arrived at their destination. Rex turned on his intercom.

"All hands to the bridge. We have an emergency. I repeat, we have an emergency," he said as calmly as he could given the situation at hand. It didn't take very long before the rest of the crew came to the bridge in various states of being awake.

"What in the hell, did you fly us into fog?" Drask said, nervous about being away from the engines for any amount of time. "It's smoke, the whole of the city is under attack and we are just seeing the very beginning of all of this," Rex said and Tayne narrowed his eyes, "Under attack by what, exactly?" he asked but didn't want to know the answer.

"Unicorns, someone sent an army of unicorns into the city, or that's all I can guess at what happened," he replied and everyone looked worried. "What in the hell is going on with you people? You sure know how to wake someone up," Calibri said, rubbing her eyes as she walked in the door. "You are not part of the crew," Unie said, who followed Tayne on to the bridge.

"You're a stupid robot and not part of any crew, so shut up," she replied and Rex had enough of the arguing.

"I don't know how the unicorns got there, but all I know is that something terrible has happened and we need to help any way we can. We need to split up and take different sectors of the city so we can get this under control. We don't know how many there are, we don't know what kinds they are so be ready for anything once we get on the ground. Do your job," Rex said and they looked at one another.

This kind of thing was unheard of for a very long time and there were many questions that needed answers.

Chapter 21

The ship hovered over the city. Buildings were on fire and smoke filled every street. The eight of them stood on the deck looking down into the nightmare.

"Well, if we're going to do something about it we should do something about sooner rather than later," Drask said and tightened her grip on the plasma rifle.

"Evie, do you have enough power to get us down to the surface?" Rex asked her.

"I think so, I feel better now," she replied and Tayne smiled. "Let me save you the trouble, see you on the ground somewhere," he said and jumped of the edge of the airship without a second thought.

"Vampires are always such show offs if you ask me, but I wish I could do that sometimes," Boz said. "No, you're just fine the way you are. Vampires may act all flashy but they horribly boring when it comes to the things that really count," Nymie replied to him and everyone pretended they didn't hear that.

"Oh, for crying out loud let me do it already, your mage is obviously broken," Calibri said, frustrated with how long this was all taking, she waved her hand through the smoke leaving a much darker swath of energy through the air and soon enough it covered all of them. Seconds later it was as if their outside world had melted away and been replaced by a nightmarish scene of fire and now screaming in the distance.

"Thanks, never thought I'd owe a necromancer twice over but thanks," Rex said and she just nodded. "Alright there is no plan here. Pick a direction and go, banish any unicorns you see and save anyone you find, but also make sure to try and get some answers because I really want to know what's going on," Rex said, took his blaster out of his holster and walked off into the smoke.

"Boz, I know you want to come with me but you need to see if you can find people alive and help them," Nymie said to him. "Yeah, I know, it's the same mission each and every time I go out on a hunt, be safe," Boz replied to her and walked off without looking back into the smoke towards the screaming.

"You really like that elf, don't you?" Drask asked her. "Yeah, he's not so bad once you get past that stupid doctor mask he always wears," Nymie replied and the painfully obvious size difference between the two of them was taking Drask's mind places it didn't want to go.

"Right, whatever. Don't get killed, I'll see you later," she said and she walked away into the smoke and the unknown. Nymie found herself alone.

Calibri was missing and the robot wasn't here either, neither was Evie. "I'm sure their fine, right, yeah. Nothing bad happened to them," she said to herself and started the hunt, trying to be ready for anything that might come out of the smoke.

Boz found it hard to see and the smoke was stinging his eyes the deeper he moved into the hellish orange glow of the city. He could feel the flames from the buildings and hoped he didn't have to deal with another Pyre horn or something worse.

Then he heard footsteps rushing up from a side alley towards his direction. Boz prepared to defend himself with his blade but quickly relaxed when he saw it was a badly burned Elroxian, she was screaming in pain. Boz immediately stopped her. "Lady what is going on? I'm a doctor and I can help you, tell me what happened," Boz said to her.

"Unicorns, more than I've ever seen just appeared an hour after the power went out. So many of them," he said as some of her scales on her left arm started to slide off. Boz widened his eyes and laid her on the ground as she was screaming. He reached in his pocket and pulled out an injector, flipped it on and pressed it against her burned skin, pressing the button.

"I am giving you a shot of nanites. I know your kind is against all this stuff but right now it's going to save your life, you need to keep as still as you can for as long as you can. I know, it's dangerous out here but you were running. I'm going to guess you were being chased by something so, sorry about this," Boz said to her and stood up despite the terror in her eyes.

"Forgive me," he said and walked backwards into the smoke, disappearing, The Elroxian woman laid there, suffering as her body was badly burnt but was slowly healing. Boz watched as the nine-foot monster stepped out of the smoke. It was another Pyre horn and Boz cursed his luck.

The thing walked and its skin cracked open revealing the fire inside of it, its eyes glowed bright orange and the horn coming out of its skull was burning with blue and white fire. Its mane, tail and hooves were also fire, it was melting the pavement as it walked. This one was acting far more normal than the last one.

"Okay matchstick, just a little closer," he said quietly and readied his electric blade for the coming attack.

Boz took a shallow breath and waited until the woman realized that the flaming horror was standing over her and the heat was making the skin on her shoulders sizzle, she began to scream. The Nanites would fix that, Boz wasn't worried but if he waited too long, she would just cook in a few more minutes.

The creature opened its maw, filled with fire and blackened teeth. It lowered its head to eat her alive, Boz leaped out of the shadows with his blade and struck the glowing blue horn at its base as hard as he could. The unicorn's head was knocked down with the blow but the horn was not severed from the skull. It flung its head back and Boz jumped back to avoid getting burned.

"Oh, come on how come that didn't work?" he said to himself and tried to think of a plan B. The woman was still on the ground. "Sorry I used you as bait but you'd better off now if you kept running and get out of sight," he said to her as she was trying to pull herself off the ground and to get away. The pyre horn's eyes flashed and it opened its mouth to unleash its hellfire. Boz took off to the left just as the cone of fire erupted from its maw. Boz didn't have time to stop running as that fire followed him closely.

Boz dived to the ground and rolled, as he did so he threw his electric sword at the beast and hit it in the chest. Instantly the cone of white fire stopped as the beast reared up in pain and surprise as its molten blood spilled out over the hilt, instantly melting it.

"Well that was a dumb plan," Boz said and while the thing was stunned. Boz took the advantage and ran away from the situation.

Without a weapon he didn't stand a chance against the thing and he was regretting his choices right now. Despite getting away he could still hear the screams of the beast behind him that didn't seem too far away.

Tayne landed on the ground on his feet and immediately looked around to make sure he didn't jump into a bad situation like an idiot. Luckily for him he appeared to be alone. Then something landed beside him and shattered the pavement sending shards in all directions. "What the hell," he said and shielded his eyes. "I followed you down," Unie said to him and Tayne was surprised that she just didn't break into pieces on impact.

"Well thanks, I don't know what we will face down here so scan the area for anything that might need our attention," he said to her and she immediately looked around. "I detect energy sources in this direction, moving away from us," she replied to him and pointed to the right. "I sense it too, but not that well so keep up if you can," he said to her and took off running in that direction.

The machine started to run as well and while not quite as fast as the vampire, she was never more than a few feet behind him.

Tayne stopped and hid behind a wall, the machine copied his movement. "Look at that, I haven't seen a Hydro on land, ever, none of this is making sense," he said to himself mostly. On the surface this unicorn was highly visible, its skin was transparent, but filled with the blood of its victims could still be seen flowing though it's body.

Underwater these were near top predators because they blended in with the water, on the land it looked as if water came to life and learned how to walk around.

It's eyes glowed blue and the horn was just as clear as the rest of it, tinted with blood. "What do we do?" she asked him. "It looks confused, it's clearly out of its element. We send it back to whatever hell it came from," he whispered and got his shotgun ready.

"I can do this," she said to him. "All you need to do is take the horn off its head and it's over, sounds pretty simple but I'd be careful if I were you," he replied and waited to see what it was doing next, but all it was doing was slowly walking down the street, confused.

"Okay, wait here. I will do this," he replied and stood up and started to walk down the street after the thing. "Hey, water horse, we need to talk," she said to the thing and it turned around as soon as it heard the words. "This is not where you belong, you need to come with me so we can send you back home and" she was cut off as it opened its mouth and let loose a high pressured stream of water. It immediately knocked her off her feet and sent her sliding all the way back to where Tayne was still waiting.

Her clothes were torn and the artificial skin was torn showing silver underneath it. It was clear the blast would have been lethal to anything living.

"Well look at that, you talked to a monster and you got blasted, who would have seen that coming?" he asked her and laughed. She sat and stood up at once.

"I will not stop," she replied and walked forward yet again. The Hydro horn towered over the machine but the water, to a machine that spent most of her time underwater was nothing more than an inconvenience. The beast narrowed its eyes at her and didn't understand, usually this was the end of the fight after a direct hit, but this time was different. If the water wouldn't work it was going to try something that would. The water unicorn started to run at the machine, but it was awkward and clumsy as it strode forward. In the water it was incredibly fast, but not here.

Unie did not move, she was incapable of being afraid. Tayne watched this and fully expected an impalement to happen at any moment. At the last second, she twisted to the side, leaped into the air and grabbed onto the horn of the beast.

She brought it down with all of the considerable weight of her metal body and snapped the horn off the beast. She stepped away and watched as the thing screamed in what looked like pain. As the blood infested water streamed from its body and it fell to the ground, dissolving into nothing. Tayne walked beside her.

"Unicorns can't die, we just sent it back home where it belongs is all," he said as the liquid horn in her hand lost its structure and splashed on the ground. "I didn't feel bad for the creature, I don't know how to do that. However, it appears to be the right thing to do," she replied to him and Tayne smiled.

"Yeah, it was. Also, that was really impressive how you did that. That water has the force to break bones on impact, good thing you're metal on the inside," he said with a smile. "Yes, let us find another one to send home," she replied and the two of them went looking for more prey.

Chapter 22

Nymie was walking down the street, but to her everything was looking the same. "Come out little unicorn, wherever you are," she said to no one. But nothing came out, nothing even was moving where she was at. "Maybe I picked the one direction where there isn't anything to find, my lucky day," she said to herself, then she stepped on something soft but it had a crunchy center as it cracked under her weight.

"Are you kidding me?" she asked and looked down, there was a human arm that used to be part of a police officer on the ground but it looked like it was cut off with a surgical tool.

"Razorhorn," she said quietly and looked around for more body parts and a trail of blood that she could follow somewhere and find this thing. She hated these monsters, out of all the more common unicorns out there, razors were the worst ones.

Nymie walked through the smoke and listened for the telltale sounds of crunching bones to detect the monster but all she could hear was fire and distant screaming. She turned a corner carefully just in time to watch another officer get sliced in half by the long, curved sword like horn of the razor unicorn from behind. There was nothing she could do to save him.

The blood sprayed over its black, sharp body and the thing grunted with a sick satisfaction. It wasn't the first time she saw something like this but it wasn't exactly something you ever wanted to get used to by any means. She quietly slipped behind the corner and out of sight while the thing was distracted by the fresh kill, it wouldn't smell her nearby with any luck.

Her plan was simple. With any luck it was going to be easy and without any problems. She passed by a window and looked inside, there was a small group of children there, scared out of their minds and she didn't think they noticed her.

She crept past the window and moved around the building as fast and as quietly as she could to get behind the razor horn. Thankfully there wasn't another nearby, she didn't think there would be however because they usually hated one another anyways. After one more corner, the beast could be seen there, feasting on its meal. She lifted her axe and took a quiet, deep breath.

Nymie lunged at the beast and swung her axe.

The blade bit into the back leg of the black skinned beast but didn't go very deep as the thing turned at the same time. The acid blood sizzled against the axe as she pulled it out. The beast roared in pain, turned around in one fluid move slashing that bladed, curved horn in her direction. Nymie barely got out of the way of the attack and narrowed her eyes.

This was part of her plan, tried and true strategy in fighting these things. The beast recovered and started to run in her direction.

"Bring it sword face," she screamed at it as it leapt through the air in her direction. She didn't back down and did the same thing. She connected her axe with the fragile, yet extremely sharp blade horn at its base. True to form and exactly as she expected, the horn shattered sending fragments in all directions.

Nymie landed on the ground face first. She rolled over and looked at the beast whose acid blood was pouring from its body in various places, eyes and mouth consuming the flesh of the monster.

"Don't come back," she said and looked down at her shoulder, one of the blade fragments was sticking out of her shoulder. She wrapped her hand in her shirt and grabbed the blade but the thing disappeared before pulling it out. There was no way to kill a razor horn without shedding some of your own blood. "Damn it," she said as her bright red blood began to flow to the ground.

"Do you need some help, miss?" a child's voice asked, afraid but still willing to venture out. "No, you should stay inside where it's safe, I'll be okay," she said, but it was no use. A young human came out with what looked like a roll of white gauze. Nymie couldn't help but laugh at this sight just a little. He was followed by a young troll and a giantess.

"What are you kids doing here anyway?" she asked as they approached. "We are on a field trip to the police station when the monsters came. Our teacher, Miss Agra went to get help but she never came back," the human boy said as he unrolled the gauze. "You weren't safe at the station?" Nymie asked her and troll girl shook her head, when Nymie took another look around, this was indeed, the police station.

"The power went out, everyone had to leave, then," she replied and looked away. "They told us to stay here," another said.

"Yeah," she said and lifted her arm to allow the boy to administer first aid. "You're very nice to help me, not too many people would bother to do this," she said. The boy was gritting his teeth, obviously disturbed by the sight of the blood but determined to finish. "Well, you fought and killed the monster, if you can do that, I can do this," he said and finished wrapping the wound as tight as he could.

"Don't worry miss, we got you," the giantess said and reached down to hold the gauze as he taped it shut.

"Thank you, I need to keep working out here and you should go back into the building to stay safe," she said to them as she stood back up. "Okay, we will, but you need to be careful out here. There are so many of these monsters and just one of you, you should stay with us," the troll girl said to her and Nymie nodded.

"I should, but I need to keep working, you keep safe and stay quiet, really quiet. I am sure you'll be fine," she said and lied, she had no idea if they would be safe or not but it was better advice than running into the smoke and dark blindly. "Okay, we can do that I guess," the human girl replied to her and without any more words returned to their hiding place inside the police station.

Nymie wondered just how many unicorns had invaded the city to make it look like this, and worse, where did they all go?

Drask was walking though the smoke choked streets when she heard a hideous noise ahead of her. "Oh come on, why me," she said quietly and pressed herself against a building nearby. Only one thing made a noise like that, a horrible, twisted and unworldly noise that chilled her despite the heat.

It was a Flesh horn, something that haunted the grim lands of the Morglands most commonly, but now one was here. This was Tayne's main prey, this was not what she wanted to deal with. The monster screamed again, closer this time. "Drask get a hold of yourself, you can do this, take the horn off just like any other Unicorn," she talked to herself, trying to calm down but the first hints of decaying flesh overpowered the smoke and it wasn't doing her any favors for her mental state.

She crept up closer to the source of the noise, the smoke began to clear away and before her stood the beast in all its decayed glory. It stood ten feet tall, its skin was pale green and falling to pieces, bits of flesh dropping on the ground. It had no eyes and the horn was an ivory white bone with strips of flesh hanging off it that looked to fresh to belong to the beast.

"Okay, you can do this, no problem," she said to herself and raised her rifle. The beast took a step but its bone hooves never touched the ground, it was walking on bodies it had gathered, not all of them were dead and now that she was closer she could hear the quiet moans of those it was saving for later. She hated these things and didn't know exactly how she was going to do it when something else was coming down the road from the left, something noisy.

Something metallic.

Drask quickly retreated and watched, to her added horror the beast she'd only seen pictures of came to the intersection. It was a War Horn, a bio mechanical monster that was more tank than unicorn. "What in the hell is it with my luck today?" she asked and could only hope for one thing to happen. She could only hope that the two beasts would end up killing one another, as they couldn't be more different and neither one was native to one another's normal stomping grounds.

The rotting unicorn turned and looked at the mechanical one as it approached, the annoyance in its body language was immediately apparent and Drask knew this wasn't where she wanted to be right now. She briefly considered helping those people who were still alive in the pile but quickly decided against it. There wasn't any hope for them. The war horn let loose a deep, trumpet like sound and the Flesh horn made no noise at all in reaction.

"Come on, fight, kill one another so I don't have to do it," she said quietly from her hiding place. The two unicorns immediately took aggressive stances towards one another. The back of the metal beast opened up and six small missiles fired out of it, straight up and they curved into the undead unicorn's direction. The abomination leapt into the missiles and took all six of them in one shot. The explosions erupted around the monster but despite its weak looking structure, it remained unharmed and the fire faded away.

The undead thing appeared to be unimpressed with this and opened its maw, green smoke poured forth from it and everything it touched immediately began to decay, rust and fall to pieces.

Some of the living people hiding in a nearby building screamed as their flesh rotted away on their still living bodies. Drask looked away and did her best not to listen or see that. It was a horrible sound she would likely never forget.

The mechanical thing didn't appear to register the threat of the corrosive and corrupt gas of the enemy and reacted too late before its thick metal legs started to rust and crack open.

The War horn, despite being damaged only walked forward at the same relentless, slow pace it had since it had arrived. "Are you insane, this thing is going to wreck you if you keep doing it like that," Drask said to herself not that she cared, she didn't want to face either of these upper level threats that each one usually required whole hunting parties to deal with.

The War horn suddenly leaped forward and sunk its five foot long metal saber for a horn deep into the undead creature's chest, whipped its head around to throw the it in Drask's direction as if it weighed nothing at all. The dwarf's eyes widened and she quickly backed up.

The thing landed on the ground long before it ever made it to her. She watched as the undead thing dissolved into mist and reformed into a standing position almost at once.

The War horn didn't seem too surprised as two Gatling guns extended from its side. Drask realized that she was directly in line with these barrels and as they started to spin she took off running out of the line of sight, around the corner of the building she was using to hide.

A second she pulled around the corner the plasma bolts began to fly. Drask turned to see the lines of green carve everything to pieces where she was standing and could only hope for the best that this is what was needed to kill the undead thing. She kicked in the door of the building and quickly made her way to the window to keep an eye on the battle, she was disappointed when she saw that the assault of plasma wasn't enough to take the monster out, or, once again even seem like it was even wounded in the slightest. "Oh, come on what's it going to take," she said out loud, and too loud.

Both of the Unicorns heard her and turned to look at the building. She immediately dropped out of sight. and quickly started to make her way back towards the door. When she was barely five feet away from freedom she heard the heavy metal footsteps of the War horn just outside and stopped.

"Damn it," she whispered to herself and turned around, to her horror the flesh horn was phasing right through the wall and its skull face and those empty eye sockets were staring right at her. Drask was terrified and ran for the stairs, it was her only choice.

She ran up the stairs, the sudden burst of activity and terror took the breath out of her in a hurry, but there was no time to try and calm down. She could hear the Unicorns downstairs one was crawling up the stairs and the other was already materializing through the floor. Drask had no idea why they just didn't kill her right away.

The window was her only chance. She didn't have time to count to three or even plan ahead. She started at a dead run and jumped through the window and hoped to make the distance to the pile of dead and wounded bodies below.

She didn't even hear the glass shatter as she went through it. All she was focused on was the pile of blood and bodies below and aimed for it.

For a few seconds everything went in slow motion, but reality and time caught up with her as he landed in the gore, sending blood in all directions.

"God damn it," she groaned and was thankful she was a Dwarf because the impact didn't break all of the bones in her body, but it did knock the wind out of her. "No time to quit, no time to bleed," she said and used her gun to help to stand up.

"Help me, please," an elf said to her weakly, he was covered by someone else and looked like he was nearly cut in half, there was nothing Drask could do about any of this.

"Listen to me, you're going to a better place, the Gods are real, haven't you heard," she said to him the only thing that came to mind, pointed her barrel at his head and fired.

She didn't look back up at the building, all she had on her mind now was to get away as fast as she could and hope they didn't track her down and started fighting one another again.

Chapter 23

On the ship, alone, the red mage sat where they left her in the room. Suddenly her chains shattered. "I am on my way, join me," a voice echoed in her head, deeply.

"I will, I will find you," she said to no one and the whole room shook. "Go to the city, wait for me," it said to her again in the thunderous voice once more. "Yes, I will," she said and the binding wards in her room burned out. Immediately she cast a teleportation spell. A second later she was on top of a tall building below the airship and looked out over the city, filled with smoke, screams and the sounds of sirens.

"They got the message, I am glad something went right for me," she said with a smile but now all she could do was wait. She was sure the wait would not be a long one.

Calex Island, or, at least where it used to be the sky above it and the ocean cracked. The binding spell containing the black energy exploded back into reality seconds later sending a great shock wave in all directions and a column of water half a mile into the air.

From the falling water a stream of black energy shot forth and burned its way towards the city so fast it was splitting the ocean into half underneath of it sending walls of water out in both directions.

The journey that took the hunters almost a day to complete was finished in mere minutes. The black comet of power slowed down and landed on the roof behind the red mage without making a sound. "It is good to see you again," he said in the same deep voice, but out loud this time. She jumped and turned around.

"Albert, you're actually alive," she said and rushed out to hug him but he stopped her, raising a hand. "I am alive, but I am not alone. The ritual worked but it was unfinished. The beast is inside me and I think I am the beast as well. I hear its thoughts in my head but also I hear my own as well," he said and looked around.

"Our children are out there, I can sense they still don't like one another. I never could solve that problem," Grayson said to nobody, walking towards the edge of the roof.

"The unicorn bomb worked. That necromancer golem we set up was perfect. The hunters sent the ship back here just like you said they would," she replied to him with a smile. "Yes, we see that it did. But now it is time to take our revenge. I will need you to witness the end of mortality on this planet so I can return the world back to before the invader gods came and played with it, watch and remember what happens tonight," Grayson said to her and stepped off the roof, falling to the ground.

"I will watch, you can rely on me," she said and didn't know what was going to happen next.

Grayson landed on the ground, breaking the pavement around him, he didn't like the way he looked so he twisted his image with a single thought. Now he was wearing a dark blue suit. "Much better," he said to himself and began to walk forward. He didn't get more than six steps before a Razor horn appeared out of the smoke. He glanced at it and his eyes flashed red.

The unicorn at once bowed its head in respect.

"That's a good kid, go now, gather the others and we shall begin the purge of mortality once and for all," he said to it, the unicorn immediately ran off into the smoke. "How did you do that?" an elf woman asked him, coming out of the shadows.

"I asked nicely. You know, unicorns really are much smarter than people give them credit for. If you treat them with respect they will do the same to you, and kill you much quicker than they might have before," he said, smiled and out of nowhere an invisible set of jaws reached down and grabbed the woman by her upper half and bit down, cutting her in half.

The torso disappeared in the air. "Oh, she was tasty, we might have to keep some of you around, you know, just in case we get bored," Grayson said with a smile and kept walking, leaving the twitching pair of legs behind him.

Rex felt something in the air change. There was a chill in it but he was sure it didn't get any colder. "What in the hell is going on?" he asked and looked around, but around here it was hard to notice if anything changed at all. Everything looked the same, ruined and burning. He picked up his communicator.

"Did anyone else feel that or was it just me?" he asked into it.

"Yeah, felt like someone walked on my grave," Nymie replied. "Ditto, where are you at, I think it'd be wise it we regrouped," Boz replied too.

"Good idea, I don't know where you're all at but we need to meet, um, let's see, where am I," he said and looked around. "Sixth and Bower, meet here as soon as you can, you shouldn't be too far away according to my tracker," he said and finished. One by one everyone said they were on their way so he decided to stand here and wait.

He couldn't help but wonder where Evie and Calibri ended up in all this mess.

He was sure they were fine, he had to tell himself that because anything else was horribly depressing.

Calibri and Evie ended up in a less than desirable place. "It's like you've never teleported before," Evie complained to her. "Hey, I'm not used to doing anyone but myself, this is what I get for helping out," Calibri replied and crossed her arms.

"Yeah, you got us stuck in the shadow realm. Do you even know what lives here?" Evie asked her as they walked along the empty, dead streets. "Yeah, necromancer here remember. I know what lives here. On the plus side we aren't constrained by energy usage. We can draw directly from here," she replied to her and Evie was not happy about this.

"So, any ideas on how to get out of here or are we just stuck, I wouldn't expect a mage school dropout like you to have any good ideas," Evie said bitterly.

"Hey, I have a few ideas but you need to think positive. This place feeds on negativity and if you get any worse you'll attract the dark walkers, or worse, so stay positive and stay invisible and best of all off the menu," Calibri replied to her and the came to a crossroads in the shadow version of the city they were in. Every single direction looked the same, black and white nightmare landscape it was turning out to be.

"I don't think there is an exit," Evie said offhandedly and the necromancer stopped walking. "Listen. I am deadly serious about the emotional output here. Suppress it, change it, do something. Keep going like this and we are both going to die. Shadow chasers use this place all the time, if they can figure it out so can we. Now start thinking of ideas, anything is better than complaining," Calibri said to her and Evie sighed.

"Shadow walkers are also insane, but maybe it has something to do with light. Look at this place. There is no light source anywhere but it's pretending there is," Evie said, looking around and Calibri noticed it too.

"Okay, let's make some light," she said and couldn't believe she was going to do this.

"So, a generic light spell sounds easy enough," Calibri said and cracked her neck.

"Let's supercharge this, let's invoke Prolexa. If we are going to do it, you should go all out," Evie said and Calibri cringed. "She's the goddess of light, but she's not exactly nice, you should read some of the stories they didn't teach in school," Calibri replied and the two of them put their hands together. As soon as they did, something on the wall behind Evie began to move.

"Damn it, it's a darkling," she said and pulled her close just as a tendril of shadow struck out in her direction. The amorphous shape slid down the wall and peeled itself off with a sickening slurp. It let loose a high pitched scream as it awkwardly walked in their direction.

"Spell later, right now we need to get away," Evie said as she looked at the thing. The two of them started to run as fast as they could, but the sound of the screams never felt as if they were getting any farther away.

"Maybe we should do the spell on the run, interested," Evie said to Calibri said and she just nodded. "Together now. Prolexia Zul Lotam Ex Juliz Mortam," the two of them recited the most powerful light spell they or anyone else knew together and above them a disk of light exploded, blinding them and turning everything around them pure white.

"Oh yeah, this was a great idea, I can't see anything," Evie said, covering her eyes but it had no effect. "Well I can't but I can smell something, it's smoke. That has to be the way out," Calibri said, took Evie's hand and the two of them started to run towards the source. The closer they got the stronger the smell became.

They ran until suddenly they could feel the moving air around them, the heat of the fire. Evie opened her eyes and adjusted to the much darker surroundings slowly.

"We made it, we're out," she said, turned and looked at the portal behind them, light still flying out of the hole in the air. "The portal will close once the light fades, it shouldn't take very long," Calibri said seconds before two black tendrils shot out and grabbed her ankles to begin pulling her back towards the portal.

Evie considered, only for a second to let her be dragged back in, but she thought better of it.

She lunged forward and grabbed onto her wrists and stopped her.

"I got you, you're going to be just fine," Evie said between straining breaths. "It's going to tear my legs off, do something else besides," she was cut off as the portal closed. The tendrils were cut off at the source and the two of them fell backwards. Evie pushed her off at once.

"See, I told you that you'd be okay," Evie said and Calibri lay on the cement. "You know I would have just let you be lunch to that thing right," she replied to her. "I doubt it, you seem like a better person than that," Evie replied and started to stand up. "I am just a very good actress," Calibri replied and stood up. "Woah, do you feel that," Evie said and looked towards the left.

"Yeah, a big kind of magic made its way to town. Not just the unicorns either. Something bigger," she replied and the two of them knew what they needed to do. Rex isn't far away. I can feel his energy and they are gathering. You can join me if you want to, but if not, I understand," Evie said to Calibri who in turn looked to the ground.

"I might as well see it out to the end, this feels bad," she replied and the two of them began to walk to where Rex and the others were meeting.

Chapter 24

It wasn't long before the others started to file in one by one to Rex's location. Drask appeared, still afraid that the monsters were following her even this far. "Holy, what happened to you?" Rex asked her, she was covered in blood and this alarmed him. "Had an encounter with a War and Flesh horn at once. Not something I wish to repeat if I can help it," she said weakly.

"Damn, you lived through an encounter with both of them, that's something to write down in the school books, killing them must have been a good feeling," Tayne said as he and Unie came walking through the smoke.

"I didn't kill them. I ran away. I'm no match for those things and you know it, one of them, maybe but not both," she replied to him still trying to calm down. "Don't blame you, you got unlucky and that seems to be a common theme with you so far," Nymie said as she appeared.

"It is, what happened to you?" Drask asked her. "Razor horn encounter. It won't be bothering anyone for a long time with any luck," she said, rubbing her arm. Boz came out of the smoke and he seemed to be just fine. "Nothing bad happened to me, I guess it is my lucky day, at least for now," he said and was worried that saying something might change things, but there was some positivity that was needed so he tried to bring it. "Where's your sword?" Nymie asked. Boz just shrugged. "Lost it in a card game," he replied.

"Well we got stuck in the shadow realm because someone didn't focus well enough in teleportation class," Evie looked at Calibri, but let it go, "But we're fine now so what did we miss and what's the plan?" she asked, everyone was surprised to see that the necromancer was still here but no one wanted to mention it.

"No real plan, I just felt weird is all and I felt like we should regroup," Rex replied to them and Evie still felt the energy.

"You're not wrong. Tayne should feel it too. Something has come into this city and it's very bad, I mean that's not a good explanation but it is bad so we should find out what it is," Evie said to them and they all agreed that was the best thing that should be done, but this energy was so pervasive that It felt like it was coming from all directions at once.

There was no way to know what way to go from here and try to find the source.

"North, west, the energy is coming from that direction," Unie said as she scanned the area.

"What, you can just know that. That's hardly fair, but very useful," Rex said with a smile and they all agreed. "Alright, so let's go find us a source of ultimate evil so we can go die. Did anyone think to call Mystic Force, or the army, or you know, anyone else on this job or is it just us today?" Boz asked and Rex shook his head.

"The force is too busy trying to keep order and the army isn't allowed into the city without royal order. As far as I know this is all on us also I don't think anyone knows how bad this is going to get, we'll be fine though. There can't be anything that horrible out there that we can't handle," Rex replied to him. "Is this the Black Unicorn?" Drask asked. "I don't know, no one knows until we see it for ourselves," Rex replied, but he was beginning to believe that the Black Unicorn was real.

The team moved northwest through the wrecked streets, the fire and the clear signs that unicorns had been here at some point. They have all since moved on, actually, there was no sign of life anywhere.

"This is a city, it shouldn't ever look like this no matter what time of the day it is," Boz said quietly as he looked around. "Yeah, but it's night, it's hard to see anything and the smoke is, oh shut up, why am I even talking about any of this," Drask said, catching herself from getting drawn into the conversation and making noise, nearly forgetting her brush with death earlier.

Boz rolled his eyes, not bothering to respond to that. "I have detected energy at least four blocks away. It is moving away, it is surrounded by multiple life forms. I do not believe we should go any further," Unie said, stopping in her tracks.

"You're right, there is something out there, something big," Evie agreed, sensing something that was giving her chills. "Well, let's see if we can take this thing back to where it belongs, we have to try," Rex said and started walking again in that direction, fearless as ever. Fear was an ally that was really hard to work with. As much as it wanted to let you know there was danger ahead, it was often way too good at its job.

Each of them did their best to keep it under control.

Grayson walked down a wide street with tall buildings on both sides of him. He was followed by unicorns of all kinds, ten in two rows behind him. Vicious things that would, on their friendliest day if such a thing existed, kill one another on sight were now passive.

"You've been destroying one another way too long. Blaming one another for the loss of your world. Each believing the other to be the enemy, the reason. You've all been tricked, it was the new gods that came and screwed it all up," he said to them and smiled.

"No matter, the time is right, the barrier has been broken, we will reclaim what is ours," Grayson said in an increasingly distorted voice.

"I get that, you've been screwed by the system. Someone stronger than you made your life miserable and everyone has to pay for it, all powerful god or a street vendor, the situation is the same," Rex said as he pushed himself off of a wall of a red building. Grayson stopped, the unicorns did as well. "Who are you, and how did you avoid detection?" he asked the man who was clearly looking to die.

"My name is, Rex and I am a Unicorn hunter. I've sent so many of those monsters back to whatever hell they came from and I did it with a smile. As for the detection thing, a cloaking spell, I wasn't sure it was going to work," he said and Grayson frowned.

"Hell is the word you used but you don't know how correct you are. It takes so much energy to escape that prison and I was buried deepest of all. The gods feared me the most so they put me where no one would ever find me, at least they hoped so, and look how that turned out," he said with a smile.

"Well I don't know what happened or why but I am going to make sure you go back, one way or another," Rex said, sighed and pulled his blaster out of his holster. Grayson started to laugh.

"You are alone, you are mortal and you should know that if I am here there is no way to, as you put it, send us back. We are home. All we need to do now is clean the world of all the pests that have invaded it," he said to Rex and the commander had to consider the possibility that this world was finished if it was true that there was no way to send the unicorns away for good.

It wouldn't stop him from attempting to try to do it anyway.

"Are you the Black Unicorn, because you really don't look like a unicorn to me. You look like a man, show yourself," Rex demanded of the creature. "You expect me to bow to your whims, you expect me to listen to someone who was created to die?" as Grayson said this he was immediately inches away from Rex's face. The commander didn't even see him move, nor did he see his hand move up to grab his throat and lift him off the ground.

"I don't think so," he said and with a flick of his hand tossed the commander through the air and into the pavement, rolling away. Despite this Rex managed to hold on to his weapon, but both of his legs were broken on impact and he was in more pain than he could remember for a long time. The others didn't need any kind of signal to attack, that was more than enough.

Drask fired her green plasma from the window she was aiming from at Grayson and the blast struck him in the side of the head, he stumbled to the right a few steps. His skin sizzled a little bit.

Tayne had his shotgun and wasted no time in getting up close and personal. He put the barrel of the enchanted shotgun against his enemy's chest and pulled the trigger. Grayson was taken off his feet but the red energy bolts fell away from him as if they were ash. Grayson landed on his feet, pushed a few inches back.

"Ouch, you guys and your toys are amusing but I do have some work to do," he said to him, smiled and with one fluid motion knocked the vampire to the side with his left hand smashing him through the air and into a third story window on the left side.

"Pests, all of you. Anyone else want to try to take a piece or are you all done now. I'd really like to know," Grayson shouted out to anyone who might listen. The unicorns were getting even more restless behind him.

"I hear you, we will go now and bring all the rest of us to this world. Patience is all you need," Grayson said to them and started to walk forward again.

Nymie leapt from the alleyway and used her axe in a surprise attack. The razor horn never saw it coming. The brittle horn shattered off of the things head and Grayson paused, winced at the sound and turned to look. The razor horn screamed in pain as its attacker backed off in a hurry. Instead of what was supposed to happen after this point, the sword blade for a horn immediately reformed on its head seconds later.

"Oh, you've got to be kidding me," she said with surprise.

"We are home. There is no place to send us back to anymore," Grayson said to her with a smile and looked up at her. "I'm going to enjoy eating you, leave her for me later, kids, we have work to do," he said and she got out of the street in a hurry.

Boz was already at Rex's side and injected him with a nano shot.

"Listen, this maniac obviously thinks he's won but he is going somewhere. We need to back off and find out where," Boz said to him and Rex, as much as he hated the idea he agreed with it. "Okay, this time we'll see what happens," he said to Boz and struggled to stand up, Boz helped him.

"Team, retreat for now," Rex said into his intercom. Grayson could only laugh as he watched Rex and the elf run out of sight in front of him. "Ignore the mortals for now, we have bigger plans to do. Don't worry however, you will get more than your fill of revenge," Grayson said to the things following him with a smile and continued walking down the road.

"Where in the hell is he going?" Evie asked the group after they found one another.

"I bet he's going to a center of magical energy to try and open some kind of rift," Calibri said and it made sense to the others.

"That thing is so impossibly strong we couldn't even touch it, so does anyone have any ideas on what to do next or do we just find a local bar and wait until the end of the world?" Drask said and she was really hoping for someone to agree, right now she could use a drink, or a whole bottle of something.

Nymie smiled at the thought, she too could use a couple of bottles of anything right about now. "As fun as a party would be we need to just follow the thing until it is getting to where it needs to be," Rex said and the others waited for the second part of the plan, it quickly became apparent that there was no second part of the plan.

"So that's it, just follow it?" Tayne said and was disappointed with this idea. "Well we don't know anything about this thing. For right now I will assume that this is the best we can do so when an opportunity presents itself we will take it," Rex replied to him.

"And if it turns out that there is none and we wasted all of our chances just following, then what," Tayne replied. Rex looked down and sighed.

"Then we all die, and none of this will matter anymore," Rex said with a smile that didn't make anyone comfortable. "Well we better go because mister supervillain is getting away," Evie said to them. The group realized they had wasted too much time talking about nothing and decided to depart. "Unie, can you still track him?" Tayne asked.

"Yes," she replied and continued. "Follow me," she finished and started to walk down the street.

Chapter 25

Evie took two steps, then everything froze. "You've been neglecting yourself," a strong voice said to her and she looked around. "What do you mean?" she asked in response and was a little bit nervous. "I mean your Aquarian star is corrupted, your skin is drying out, you're dying and you won't be any use to your team dead. This is why your energy is failing you and why you ended up in the shadow realm," the voice said to her and a hand came down on her shoulder.

"Let me help you again," he said and walked around her. It was Elrox. He snapped his fingers and her Aquarian star pendant began to glow, immediately she did feel better. With everything that was going on she didn't even realize how weak she was.

"Thank you, we need your help," Evie said to the God and he just smiled.

"The black unicorn is a plague on our land. There are many things that are plagues and vast secrets that would, for now, be better left unsaid. But I will tell you this. We did not imprison the unicorns. Mortals did. Thousands of years ago you worked together and you managed to do it. The unicorn believes we helped, but all we did was provide guidance, as I will do for you now," Elrox said and crossed his arms.

"The unicorn's body is still trapped. Its mind and power is free. It will need to unite and in order to do that a portal will be opened, you will know your chance when you see it presented to you," Elrox said with a smile then time restarted once again.

"Hey, Evie, are you okay?" Drask said waving her hand in front of her eyes. "Yeah, I mean, I'm fine," Evie said, shaking her head. "So, what would I tell you if I was just visited by a God and he seemed pretty sure we could win this," she said and started walking again.

"Did they give you any super powers or plans on how to win or did they just say good luck," Drask asked her. "Basically, said good luck and sent me on my way," Evie replied and smiled for the first time in a while, despite everything she was finally feeling closer to her old self again.

"Well the next time you talk to a god, make sure to ask for some holy rocket launchers or something," Drask said and walked to catch up with the rest of them. "Yeah, I'll do that," she replied.

Rex and the others followed their prey, but made sure to keep their distance. Rex was sure that Grayson knew where they were, or at least that they weren't going to give up so easily. Evie made her way up to Rex, avoiding the others.

"Elrox said that Gods didn't trap the unicorns, people did. Said that the body is still trapped. They have to unite and he said that we'd know our chance when we saw it," she said to him and he nodded.

"Information that could have been useful before I got both of my legs broken for nothing, but alright. Did he happen to mention what this chance would look like or anything else that could be useful," he asked her and Evie just shook her head.

"You know how the gods get, they don't like to be too direct in their affairs. They like to be weird," she replied and Rex rolled his eyes. "Useless as always. Listen. We're all tired and worn out. Do you think you could cast a regeneration spell on us so, when we get to where ever we are going we will be ready to fight at least," Rex asked her and Evie nodded.

"Yeah, I can do that. No problem," she said and walked away.

Evie lifted her staff up and held it in both hands. Unexpectedly, a bright blue, and warm light washed over all of them. "What in the hell," Drask said shielded her eyes as the rest of them did the same. In seconds, however, they all began to feel better despite their drained physically and emotional state.

"A regen spell, really. We aren't that far gone you know," Nymie complained about it. "Don't worry about it, think of it as a safety net," Evie replied to her, set her staff down and keep walking in the same direction. "I don't feel any different," Tayne said, disappointed.

"That's because you're a vampire and the only thing that keeps you moving is blood, speaking of do you need some," Caibri said, walking beside him. "Are you offering or what?" Tayne didn't like necromancers but he'd settle for eating one right now.

"Bite the troll, she's got plenty of blood and Troll blood makes the undead things stronger," she said to him and Tayne was reminded of how he felt the last time. "Nymie, I have a question," Tayne said to her and she turned and looked at him.

"What is it?" she responded. "Can I bite you again, I mean, I could find a random but that might seem a little bit weird," he replied to her and she shrugged. "Okay, just don't take too much," she said and held out her right arm. Tayne sighed he didn't want to do this again but it was his best option right now. He walked up to her thick, green arm and sunk his fangs into it. Nymie winced in pain as she felt her blood being drained. Boz winced and had mixed emotions about seeing this and decided to stop watching. Tayne's eyes widened.

Tayne forced himself off Nymie's arm and stepped away. She looked as the bite marks closed at once, still under the effects of the regeneration spell, she didn't feel drained this time.

"Troll blood is addictive, it's used in the Morgland black markets by all kinds of evil people. You're worth, literally, billions of in all kinds of currency to the right buyer," Tayne said and Nymie had no idea.

She'd never really been worth anything beyond being a Unicorn hunter.

"Well anyone who wants to get a hold on her is going to have to go through me first," Boz said and grunted. Drask and Nymie laughed at him, but Boz kept his serious tone.

"I trust you, little elf," Nymie said and Rex suddenly stopped because Unie did. "Our target has stopped, he is standing near Nyrad Tower, the school for mages," the machine said to them and both Evie and Caliban's eyes went wide. "It makes sense he'd be here, it's on an energy node one of several in the city," Caliban said, worried at what this might mean.

"This is the best spot for what we need to do," Grayson said as he stood in front of Nyrad Tower, and in front of the tower mages dressed in various, bright colored robes stood to protect their school. "You are not welcome here," the Elroxian mage said in a loud voice as he stood his ground and continued.

"Leave now and you will not be harmed," he finished and Grayson tilted his head.

"You are amusing, but I don't think you or anyone else can stop me, you can try but I should warn you. I have the power of a god, literally," Grayson replied and started walking forward. The mages lifted their staffs in unison and fired bright rays of light, fire and various other destructive magic spells in his direction. Grayson raised his right hand as they impacted him.

The intruder was engulfed in burning light that blotted him out. The mages raised their weapons, their energies increased as the rays grew stronger. To their surprise, the tangled mess of magic began to move towards them.

"The ages haven't been kind to you. I remember the days when a single elf mage could fight me to a draw, but it appears numbers are no substitute for true power," Grayson said in a voice that seemed to come from all directions at once, and soon after there was a shockwave that blasted out sending the energy out in all directions knocking all the mages straight to the ground.

"No please, don't get up on my account," he said and raised his hands. Black beams of energy blasted the fallen, would be protectors. On impact their bodies crumbled away to ash that was quickly blown away.

"Good, now, I need to do one last thing. No one gets in. Surround the building and keep it safe until I am finished," Grayson said to them and the unicorns began to surround the building. Grayson walked up the steps and the doors opened for him as he approached.

"Excellent, now it's time to return to the good old days," he said as he walked inside the building.

"Well, he just took out a good number of very skilled mages in one shot, does anyone have any good ideas of what to do next or is the bar idea still a thing we can do?" Drask asked, more than ready to let this come to an end.

"Will you shut up about that already, I imagine he needs protection because he's going to be weak. The amount of energy to bridge the worlds is insane, even if you're a god, and if we can get to him during that time I think we can win this," Evie said and Rex narrowed his eyes. Calibri was nodding. "I was just going to say that myself, the fish mage is catching on," she said sarcastically.

"How are we getting past the unicorns, then, anyone have any great ideas?" Drask asked, knowing full well that you couldn't just teleport into a mage school and get away with it.

"We can fly," Rex said to them and Calibri nodded. "That could actually work. Mage schools are protected against magical intrusions, I don't see why we couldn't just fly to the top," she said and Nymie sighed. "I wonder why mister unicorn god didn't just fly?" Boz asked Evie just glared at him. "Didn't you listen to me?" she asked.

"I hate flying, but if it's the only way I guess that'll be what we need to do," she said and Evie knew just the spell that would work. "This is the point of no return. You can turn back now if you want to but if we live know that I will make sure everyone knows you gave up at the end," Rex said with a smile.

"Nothing like a little blackmail to get the morale up," Boz replied and took a deep breath. "I thought so, now we need to make sure that we have no plan, if we are predictable that thing up there will know it, Evie, get us up there," Rex said and his logic didn't make sense to anyone right now.

"Hulota" she said in her native language and at once all of them were flying off the ground. Evie was controlling the direction and for this Nymie shut her eyes. She hated magical flight and the others were grateful, flying on your own power if you've never done it was extremely difficult. The group, in mere seconds were already over the building they were using for cover. The unicorns never even bothered to look up.

The group sailed right over their heads in complete silence and quickly rose up the side of the tower, close to the side so they could blend in with the dark. They didn't need some onlooker gawking and drawing attention to them either.

They landed on the top of the building as Evie killed the spell. Grayson, surprisingly had not arrived yet. "Alright, everyone let's get behind the access door so he doesn't see us standing here like idiots," Tayne said and started running towards the door, the others followed his lead.

"I like this non plan we have going on here, I hope we can pull this madness off so we can let the rescue teams move in and go home," Drask said and Rex punched her in the arm. "Quiet, suppress your inner moron for a few minutes, alright," he said to her and she shot a glare in his direction, he didn't pay attention to her in the slightest.

The access door opened and he walked forward on to the roof.

"I really expected to be met up with a bunch of heroes up here for one last stand. I guess the unicorns actually did manage to fend them off, my lucky day," he said and took a deep breath as he walked to the center and sighed.

"Okay, I know you're there, you can come out," he said without turning around.

Nymie just about stood up to confront him when Rex immediately, and with strength she didn't know he had pulled her back down and shook his head. "Really, I mean, is there really nobody up here but me, this is usually the part the hero shows up," Grayson said and shrugged. "Cool, I guess I can just get this over with," he said and his hands began to burn with bright orange and black fire.

He lifted them into the air and fired two beams into the sky. Above him the biggest portal any of them had ever seen began to form. "The bridge will never be broken again, I will free all of you and together we will rule this world. Come out my friends, join me in paradise," he screamed into the growing, spinning black cloud vortex above them.

"Attack now?" Tayne asked and Evie shook her head no. Tayne rolled his eyes he knew that if they waited much longer there wouldn't a world left to protect.

Grayson's human body began to glow bright orange, then a massive beam came out of him and flew into the portal only for a few seconds. He fell to his knees but out of the portal, streaks of fire started to fall to the earth.

"Now," Evie said and Tayne was the first to react. He jumped out of the shadows and bashed Grayson in the back of the neck knocking him face first into the floor.

"What in the hell," Grayson said as he at once rolled over and kicked Tayne away from him. He was nowhere near his previous power but he lifted up straight up off the ground vertically to stand up and punched Tayne in the face, knocking him into the air and off the edge of the roof.

"Once my body gets here I'll kill all of you nice and slow, but I have all the time in the world and you'll never keep up with me!" Grayson screamed over the rising wind and ran for the edge of the roof and jumped. He jumped into the air and slammed into a shield and was knocked back at once into the roof.

"What is the meaning of this?" he asked as he picked himself up. Rex just shrugged, he didn't know either. "I figured you'd try to run so as soon as we got here I put up a shield," Calibri said, Rex and Boz were impressed with her foresight.

"Well, what about Tayne then?" Drask asked. "Normal shields like this don't work so well with the undead, I'm sure he's already on his way back up," Evie replied to her and focused back on the task at hand.

"Let's kill this bastard so we can get things back to normal," Rex said, and fired his weapon at Grayson. The beam hit the thing in the chest and he staggered back two steps but didn't fall.

"We get it, save us the you're stronger than all of us together speech," Boz said as he rushed forward. "Tyon," Evie screamed and a replica of his old electric blade appeared in the elf's hand. Without thinking and with his electric blade in hand, he swung at his neck. Grayson raised his right arm and blocked the blade. The sparks were flying but he didn't get cut.

"Then you should have picked a better weapon that didn't make you have to get so close to me," he replied and pushed against the blade flinging him away with ease.

Boz hadn't felt a strength like that in his life he and knew if he tried to resist it he'd be dead so he jumped at the same time and allowed the force to take him away from the battle. Nymie caught him before he could hit the shield.

"I owe you," he said as she sat him down with one arm. She didn't respond as her and Drask moved in for the attack. She fired a green blast that hit him in the face. He was fast but not fast enough to avoid plasma. Pieces of his flesh were blown off on impact and he grabbed his face as smoke rose from the wounds.

Nymie rushed forward and sunk her axe deep into the left shoulder of the thing, she was aiming for the neck but he twisted at the last second. Grayson charged and grabbed her by her waist. He picked the eight foot woman straight up off the ground with one punch to the stomach to throw her away.

He pulled the axe out of his shoulder as she hit the ground and cracked the roof. "You troll, you'll die for that," he said in a barely understandable voice due to most of his face being torn off.

He pulled the axe up but was stopped by a pair of hands. "What?" Albert asked, surprised. Unie had waited for the best time to attack and she decided it was now. She used the leverage to pull him on to his back with ease and put her foot on his wrists holding him on the ground. Tayne came crawling over the edge of the building finally as Nymie groaned and struggled to get up.

"My memory banks remember you. You made me open the shield, you made me responsible for killing all of the villagers, you must be punished," she said, almost with a hint of anger in her voice.

"You're just a machine, not dead, not alive. Just wires meant to do what you are told," Grayson snarled and twisted away from her to stand up only to be punched in the face by Rex just as he did so making him stagger back again.

"This machine has more right to exist than you do," Rex said and nodded to Evie and Calibri. The two of them blasted the man with rays of bright yellow light. This time Grayson screamed as his human form began to dissolve where it stood. Drask took aim, switched her rifle to its kinetic mode and pulled the trigger sending a solid beam into Grayson. Grayson's body burst into yellow and purple fire as it fell to its knees, still screaming.

"You suppose that's enough? If it is closing the portal should take place at any time because I think I see something at the end of this tunnel and it's not light,"

Tayne said as he looked up into it. He could swear he saw what looked like a massive horse head in the darkness.

"Yeah we should bring this to an end," Nymie said, agreeing with the vampire. Grayson was now just a pile of fire and human shaped ash and bones now. There was no sign of life from him anywhere.

"Ladies, it's up to you, I'll trust you but we should, you know. Make a choice because if we don't we're going to die," Rex was getting nervous about this whole situation and the Mage and Necromancer cut off their attack.

"This is as good as over," Evie said and Calibri nodded. The two of them turned their attention to the sky. The shield disappeared in an instant. "Just like before, we work together and take this thing out. We can do it," Evie said to her unlikely partner and they both closed their eyes.

White and blue beams erupted from their fingertips and the top of her staff. Everyone watched as the lines of light began to swirl around the portal in the opposite direction and the whole thing began to flow in the direction of the light.

"Yeah, that's how you do it, lock this thing up," Drask said with a smile, the first real smile she had in a long time.

The others watched the event unfold, the portal began to shrink down and the streams of fire stopped entirely now. "It won't be long now, this nightmare is going to be over," Rex said with a smile and just then he realized that nobody was paying attention to

Grayson, just because he appeared to be dead didn't mean he really was.

Rex turned around and found Grayson's skeletal, charred face standing inches away from his. His empty eye sockets burning with purple light.

"You think you can just undo everything I have done?" he said with an inhuman, horrifying voice that he didn't have before. Rex tried to jump back but Grayson reached out and grabbed his arms. Rex twisted away and kicked the burning skeleton away from him. Grayson hit the ground in a mangled pile of flame and bones, but quickly pulled himself back up.

Rex rushed the thing and shot it in the head blasting chunks of bone in every direction. Grayson didn't seem to notice and stood up again. "I'm going to peel the flesh off of your bones and make you watch as I eat you," the charred thing screamed in a broken voice.

"Too bad for you I taste really bad, you're no God, you're just another dwip who needs to die," Rex replied to him and lunged for the attack, shooting the false god in chest again. While the physical damage was clear, it was already regenerating. Rex knew that nothing he could do to the thing would be enough. Now there was only one other option.

"They are going to close that portal, and then we will find a way to put you down forever. And think about it, if the Black Unicorn's power is trapped here, away from its body. How do you think all the other unicorns are going to feel about you then?" he asked with a smile.

Grayson had been distracted from the mages work, the portal in the sky had been closed considerably and his connection to the source of the power was almost gone.

"Fine," he said and torn up mouth turned into a smile.

"If I can't have this world back, I will at least have you to keep me company in mine," he said and his skeletal jaws twisted into a smile. Albert ran forward and grabbed Rex by the neck, then he took off flying towards the portal.

Nymie was able to grab onto Grayson's leg seconds before it was too late. "Guys, help me," she screamed and the others quickly rushed to her aid. They all grabbed onto Grayson and held him in place, but despite all of their strength, he was slowly pulling away.

"Guys. The portal is closing. I doubt any prison on earth can hold him once he's fully regenerated. You need to let me go, this needs to happen. I'll do my best to make sure he won't screw with anyone else ever again," Rex yelled out to the others.

The portal was nearly closed.

"This is an order, let me go, now," Rex yelled out and Grayson laughed at the order. "Damn you, Rex," Drask said and let go. The others did too. "Blast us into the portal," Rex yelled as they did and twisted around in the air. With Grayson exposed, the team fired and hit their mark.

With the shield dropped, Grayson struggled to get free, but Rex held him fast as weapon's fire pushed them forward. Rex was doing everything he could to hold on to the struggling thing in his arms.

They were forced into the shrinking black mass in the sky just as the shield dropped. Seconds later it disappeared. As soon as it had begun, it was all over, at least this part of it. Evie and Calibri stopped their magic and nearly collapsed. Tayne and Drask were there to keep them from falling over.

"Do you suppose he's dead?" Boz asked, breaking the silence. "Don't you even think that, not for a minute," Nymie replied, holding back the tears over what just happened.

Chapter 26

The others stood there, not knowing what to do next or where to go. Suddenly the sounds of gunfire and magic blasts came from the streets below. It attracted their attention so they walked to the edge of the tower and sat down.

"It looks like the King finally called in the army to deal with the rest of the unicorns," Tayne said and the others watched as they could see war walkers blasting energy at the unicorns. They saw a horn shatter and could only smile as the thing did what it was supposed to and disappeared into nothing.

"I am glad things are back to the way they used to be," Drask said and sighed.

"Woman, things won't ever be the same after this. Look at the city, its ruined. There is no telling how many people died in the attack," Calibri replied, Drask groaned.

"Shut up, Necromancer," she replied.

"One time I needed his help with a Flesh horn out in the Morglands. Rex, I swear it's true, he used a dead body as cover to literally walk right up to the thing and broke its horn off with his bare hands. Then he looked at me and said, what, are you okay, like it was no big deal," Tayne laughed, sharing one of the stories he had with him to try and lighten the mood.

"The man was an impressive hunter, what do you say we meet up here this time next year in memorial. You know, if we're still alive and all," Boz said to them and for a few seconds there was silence.

"If they let us up here I'll be here," Evie said with a knowing smile, she was sure it wouldn't be a problem. She turned to look at Calibri. "What about you, you did really well these past few days," she asked her and Calibri sighed.

"I never thought myself as being a talented unicorn hunter but sure, I'll be here. I liked the guy. He was cool," she said and Evie smiled. "Yeah, he was, and still is. I think we can save him, but I'll need some time," she said to the others but none of them were interested in raising their hopes.

In this job hope was something that would either get you killed or drive you insane.

"Come on, let's report back to the castle so we can finish this," Drask said to them and one by one they started to stand up. "Can we fly back down? I don't think I want to see what that monster did to the inside of this tower," Boz said, having seen enough death and destruction.

For once no one complained. Evie casted the spell, despite her loss of energy and the group slowly floated back to the ground. It wasn't long before they landed and began to make their way back to the castle and avoiding the military and their battles.

The group stood in the water filled throne room. King Lexam sat on the throne looking over the people who had just saved his kingdom, and likely the world.

"Sacrifice is often what is needed to make a good thing happen, our legends of the past are filled with larger than life heroes giving everything and today the children will know of a new legend. How Commander Rex was willing to give it all up to save us all. May the gods protect him where ever he is," Lexam said and sighed, not getting out of his chair.

The group knew better than to say anything. "Thank you," he said to all of them and smiled. Lexam swam out of his throne and stood on the floor.

"If you want anything, just ask. You've saved us all and it's the least we can do to reward you. If you want anything, ever, just ask," he said to them with a glint in his eye. The line of people remained silent. Then Calibri stepped forward. "I would request one thing," she said to him and Lexam, expecting them to want nothing in return looked at the young necromancer.

"What would you like?" he asked her as he walked over.

"We necromancers are seen as an evil people, and there are some of us who are really insane. But we are not all that way. I would ask for a diplomatic channel be opened up. I don't want to be feared for a choice

I made, and I don't want my people to be hated. I believe we can start making things better," she said to him, nervous because Calibri knew that he could have her killed in an instant.

"Done," Lexam said with a smile.

"You're the ambassador now between our people. It won't be easy but I believe the Delrax Necromancers and the Elroxians can get along. What is peace for if not everyone can enjoy it?" he said and nodded. "Anyone else need anything. You've more than earned your reward. If you can't think of anything now please, feel free to come back at any time. The offer stands forever," he said and crossed his arms, continuing.

"In the meantime, I grant you the highest award I can give," Lexam said. He snapped his fingers Silver Coral medal pendants appeared around their necks.

"Go now, take some time off," he said to them and swam back to his throne, sitting down. The began to kneel but he stopped them.

"You saved me, no need to kneel or bow to me or anyone else in the kingdom ever again," he said and smiled. "Let's get out of here this is getting weird," Nymie whispered and Tayne smiled. "Yeah I'm with you," he said under his breath.

The group walked towards the airlock to get out of the castle and in minutes they were back in the air, in the main hall.

"So, this is it, I guess we go home now," Drask said and seemed sad about it. "Hey, no need to worry. We're only a phone call away," Boz said and smiled.

"Well if you don't mind I am taking Unie home with me. She doesn't have a place to go back to," Tayne said and everyone raised their eyebrows.

"What?" Tayne asked, oblivious.

"Nothing, don't worry about it. Well, it's been fun but I hope I don't see any of you for a long time," Calibri said with a smile and disappeared into a black column of smoke. Evie smiled. "I need to meditate in my chambers for a week after this. If you need a mage, you have my number. I'll keep you posted about Rex when I find something," Evie said and with a tap of her staff was gone in a beam of bright blue light.

"See you at the memorial, don't take it personal but I don't think I'll need your help any time soon," Drask said with a smile, put her rifle over her shoulder and walked off. She did her best to look calm but her encounter with the two terrifying unicorns left her shaken to the core and she wasn't sure she could do this job anymore.

Tayne and Unie walked off in the same direction. Tayne waved as he took a left turn and disappeared out of a door opposite of Drask.

Boz looked at Nymie. "Your place or mine?" he asked her, after coming so close to death so many times, he decided that this wasn't a hard thing to ask anymore and Nymie vaguely remembered what a mess her place was. "Yours," she said and the two of them walked out together.

Marion was sitting at home when the power came on late at night. Ten minutes after that, the phone rang and she picked it up. Rex wasn't back yet and she hadn't heard from him since the last call to try to get her to leave. The ring had a bad feeling to it. "Hello," she said into the phone.

"Yes, Marion. I have some bad news, so, I'll just come out and say it. Rex is missing. He was thrown into the portal to another world to save us all," the voice on the other end of the phone said and he almost knees gave out on her, the news was devastating.

"I'm sorry, but we'll do everything we can to find him," the voice said and Marion was in shock.

"Okay, I, I'll wait for you to call," she said and hung up the phone. She looked out the window, the coffee Rex drank out of was still on the counter from before he left. She wasn't sure why but she didn't have the willpower to get rid of it. She walked to it, picked it up and dumped the coffee down the drain.

"Damn it, why did you have to give yourself up like that, wasn't there a better way?" she asked herself and just then she could have sworn that she felt a phantom hand rest on her shoulder and a distant voice trying to call out only for a second, but when she looked around nothing had actually changed.

"I'm already losing my mind," she said sadly and slumped into a chair.

The reality of the situation hadn't dawned on her yet, the shock was still numbing the pain of not knowing what actually happened. Even though the announcer on television droned on about a Unicorn dirty bomb attack in the capital, in her mind, a plan of her own was beginning to form to get her husband back from whatever hell he had banished himself.

About the Author

My name is Jesse Wilson. I live in South Dakota and I am 36 years old.

I am also a lifelong Godzilla fan.

A long time ago, I realized that the world inside my head was more appealing than the world I lived in on a day to day basis most of the time and real life was something I was never particularly good at. There was always something missing and I never seemed to find it.

I had dabbled in the art of writing since as long as I can remember. Silly stories that never really amounted to anything, while most people give this up and move on, I just kept moving forward. Never stopping, by the time I was 13 years old I had managed to create my first Godzilla fan fiction stories. None of them were that great, but not too many people are at the beginning of anything.

At 15 had started to role play online, free form role playing, they called it. This is where I learned how to show things and not just tell them. This was way before the online games they have today. For fun I used to help other people create their character profiles, I got rather good at it, too. This is where I became addicted to writing.

I wrote my first "novel" when I was 16 years old in High school, it started out as something I just wanted to try, but the thing ended up saving me in English class when I told the teacher and she allowed me to turn the thing for extra credit. I still don't know how that ended up working, but it did. I managed to turn the thing into a trilogy before I graduated high school.

Unfortunately, the whole thing was lost when a storm rolled through, teaching me the importance of backing everything up.

After graduation I just got a job and committed myself to "real life" everything that wasn't needed took a back seat, writing included.

In 2006 I rejoined the online world of roleplaying and rediscovered why I liked to do it. From 2006 to 2010 I managed to create one of my favorite characters, Bob the Supervillain.

In the summer of 2010, I began the thing that would unknowingly become an epic. The Delta Squad series, inspired by the people I worked with at the time. It started out as two thousand word drop in the bucket. By the time 2013 came along, the series had evolved into a thirteen-book series! However, it was all a hobby. Something I wanted to see how far I could take it.

2013 was a major turning point in my life. I contracted a near lethal MRSA infection. I was in the hospital for three weeks and almost didn't make it. Up until then I had just decided to "do my best to get by," facing death in such a painful way and making it this time, made me want to try a little harder. I decided that I would do my best to get the Delta Squad books published. Not self-published, but actually done by a real company.

However, I wanted to do more. Delta Squad was my main project but writing offered so much more. So, I dived into the world as deeply as I could. I discovered NaNoWriMo in 2015 and gave it a shot. I've done it three times and won each time, I'm happy to say.

In 2016 I discovered Kaiju fiction was actually a thing. So, I wanted to try my hand at it. I created a monster called Narbosaurus! Everyone I told the name to, thought it was one of the worst names they had ever heard, and idea too, even though I never revealed very much.

So, I wrote it anyway, edited it the best I could and sent the thing in. My very first book I had ever sent in. I had no expectations. To my surprise they accepted it! My very first book was accepted, the thing everyone I had told in advance had said was a bad idea, it worked out way better than I hoped it would.

Now, in 2018 I hope to see my writing career go further than I ever thought possible, and with time I know this will just be the first steps into something truly amazing.

Commander Rex and the Black Unicorn
ISBN: 978-4-82414-077-7 (Mass Market)

Published by
Next Chapter
2-5-6 SANNO
SANNO BRIDGE
143-0023 Ota-Ku, Tokyo
28th July 2022

www.ingramcontent.com/pod-product-compliance
Lightning Source LLC
LaVergne TN
LVHW032009070526
838202LV00059B/6359